A KEY WEST CHRISTMAS
A Sweet Clean Christmas Romance

BARBARA MCMAHON

1

Shelly stood in the doorway, champagne bottle in one hand, two flutes in the other, staring at her boss. Correction, soon-to-be-former boss. How many times had she walked into his office and seen him standing exactly there, gazing out the window at the Manhattan skyline?

Beau Charlmers was a tall man who wore his Italian business suits with flair. His dark hair was cut short. He was clean shaven, trim and fit, and in excellent shape. Too young to give it all up she believed. Yet today was his last day in the office. Tomorrow he was officially retired.

She'd seen him like that too many times to count. It was his go-to thinking position. But today was the last time. What would he do when he needed to think in the future? There was no amazing view of New York from a sail boat.

Nine years. It'd been a wild ride. She'd learned so much. And become more proficient than she ever imagined back on the day she started. Then she'd been a fresh graduate from college with a business degree and full of lofty goals.

She glanced out the window. It was snowing lightly. Soon the city would be covered in sparkling white. The forecast was for flurries only. No worry about getting home.

She stepped inside the office, the flutes clinking slightly.

Beau heard and turned. Smiling he glanced at the champagne.

"Are we celebrating?" he asked.

"We are. One last toast to the future. I'll miss you," she said easily.

It was an effort to keep her tone light. She'd miss him so badly it was like cutting off a part of her. Not that she'd ever let him know the full extent of her feelings for him. She prided herself on her professionalism.

For the last nine years they'd been together every day during the week and many weekends. They'd traveled the world for business. She'd visited places others envied. Met illustrious people and a few not known for honesty or integrity. She'd skied in Switzerland, snorkeled off the sparkling waters of Fiji, and eaten specially prepared meals in India.

Beau had been a demanding boss—yet more than fair and generous. Her compensation had grown each year as she became more and more of an asset to his growing empire. He'd already made his first millions by the time he hired her. Now he'd topped off into the billionaire category.

She put the flutes on the empty desk. Handing him the bottle to open, she glanced around the office. All his pictures, commemorations and commendations had been removed and packed away. The few statues that had been displayed on the shelves were gone. The office looked cold and sterile.

Tomorrow someone else would occupy this corner office—Lyle Jefferies. Newly named as CEO for the firm, his goal was to take the company to new heights.

Shelly wished him well.

She wouldn't be here to see it.

The cork popped and Beau swiftly filled their glasses. He lifted his as Shelly reached for hers.

"To the future," he said. "May all your dreams come true."

She smiled and touched the rim of his glass with hers.

"May all your dreams come true."

Sipping the excellent vintage she was suddenly

overwhelmed with emotions. She swallowed hard. She'd come this far, she could stay in control a little longer. She prayed she could.

The end had come. In a few minutes she'd say good bye. It was highly unlikely she'd ever see him again. The thought pierced her heart. But she'd soldier on, never giving him reason to suspect the monumental crush she'd had on him all these years.

He'd sold his home in the Hamptons, sublet his apartment in town. The next few days would have him winding up any personal aspects not yet addressed, then he'd step aboard his sailboat in preparation to sail down the east coast, through the Panama Canal and on to explorations in the Pacific. His plans had been made. He wasn't even forty but was turning his back on business to relax and see what else life had to offer.

"Thanks for the ride," she said, working to keep her voice light. "It's been amazing."

"You did more than your share. I'd never have gone as far without you."

His smile had her insides turning mushy.

She prided herself on being the sophisticated personal assistant to one of the world's richest men. New York had been her home for nine years. She was not some teenager with hormones all over the place. Swallowing hard, she mustered a smile and ignored the dancing butterflies in her stomach. Ignored the sting of tears.

"You've been invaluable," he said, taking another sip of the champagne. "I'll miss you, Shelly. Lyle may have a new direction to take the company, but that doesn't mean it won't be as exciting as we've had."

She kept her smile in place and emptied her glass. Putting it down on the table, she glanced outside again. Then back at Beau.

"I'm not staying," she said.

"What?"

He looked stunned. It took a lot to startle a master of negotiations who never gave away his thoughts. She knew her news was a shock. She should have told him earlier, but the time never seemed right. Now, right time or wrong, she'd share her plans.

"Your decision to see the world on your terms gave me the kick I needed. I've decided I want a change. I'm tired of cold New York winters, of crowds that seem to grow year after year. I want to work where I can wear flip-flops every day, never have to wear a heavy coat or fight the crowded subway."

"I didn't know you were unhappy here," he said slowly, placing his glass on the desk.

"I haven't been unhappy exactly–most of that due to you. With your leaving, I've made up my mind to try something different. Be someone different. Nothing against Lyle, but if I'm not working with you, I'm going in a new direction."

"And that is?"

"Key West. I've accepted a job as concierge in a high end hotel right on the beach."

"A concierge?" He frowned. "Hotel workers don't get paid that much."

"I don't need the money. The investments you've recommended over the years pay nice dividends. With freedom from financial worries, I can work at what makes me happy."

"I can't see you as a hotel worker," he said slowly, as if the concept was too foreign to believe.

"If it doesn't work out, I'll still have my skills and experience to find another job. But I'm really looking forward to this. So while you enjoy skimming along the ocean waves, think of me on the beach in Key West."

"When do you leave?" he asked.

"Two weeks from tomorrow. Just in time for Halloween at the beach."

2

Fourteen months later.

He'd found her. Beau Charlmers stood to one side of the cavernous lobby looking across to where the concierge desk was surrounded by skimpily-clad vacationers. He'd been in Key West three days, checked out several other high-end hotels and found her here in the Royal Key Resort.

He almost didn't recognize her. His sophisticated PA from New York no longer wore a tailored dark suit with a white blouse. Instead the colorful sarong she wrapped around herself displayed beautiful tanned shoulders. Her hair was loose around her shoulders, wavy in the humid air—not pulled back into a low ponytail, sleek and tamed. He couldn't see her feet. Was she wearing the flip-flops she'd longed for?

She laughed at something one of the young men who were plying her with questions said. Beau was startled at how young and happy she looked. Not that he'd ever suspected she wasn't happy in New York, but he tried to remember seeing her laugh so freely before.

He'd wait until the guests left and she was alone. He suspected she'd be surprised to see him.

It'd been more than a year since they'd said goodbye in his office. He thought back to how startled he'd been to hear of her leaving New York. Somehow he'd never pictured her anywhere but working for Farmingham Investments.

When the last of the guests turned, he took a step forward.

"Beau Charlmers? Whatever in the world are you doing here?" a voice called from his left.

He turned and Elizabeth Wilson took two steps closer and reached out to clutch his arm.

"I haven't seen you in ages. Last I heard you'd given up on New York and set sail to see the world. What are you doing in Key West?"

"Hi, Elizabeth. It's a stop on seeing the world," he said, glancing over his shoulder to Shelly.

She was busy writing something. He didn't think she'd seen him. Impatiently he turned back to Elizabeth and tried to catch up to what she was saying.

"...in the bar. He'd love to see you. Join us for

a drink and tell us all about where you've been and how long you're here. You've missed some great parties in New York."

"I'd like to see your father, but I have somewhere I need to be," he said, glancing back at Shelly.

She was gone. The concierge desk was empty.

"No, I insist. Surely you have time for a moment. Dad will be so delighted to see you. He still talks about the Mets game you two attended how many years ago?"

Beau nodded, remembering the outing he'd arranged for several high-end customers. Everyone had a great day–made even better with the Mets' win.

"Just for a minute, I really need to get going," he said, wondering if Elizabeth would let go of his arm as they walked toward the bar situated to the side of the main lobby. Open to the sea breezes, the area was only partially full.

"Jason, good to see you," Beau said when they reached the man nursing a drink at one of the tables near the opening.

"Beau Charlmers, you're the last person I'd expect to see here. How are you?"

The older man rose and shook hands, smiling at his daughter.

"I'm sure Elizabeth's happy to see you, too. She gets a bit bored hanging out with an old man like me."

"Oh, Dad, not so. But it's good to see Beau, isn't it?"

She snuggled just a little closer.

"Join us for a drink?" Jason invited.

"I'm on my way somewhere. Maybe another time. Are you two here for long?" Beau said.

"For another few days. A friend of mine is getting married on the beach. A long-held dream of hers. Do your remember Suzzie Baker?" Elizabeth asked.

Beau nodded once. One of the many women he'd known in New York. Always up for clubbing, parties and social activities that filled their days.

"She's marrying Bart Herman. They met at a New Year's Eve party and fell in love, so romantic," Elizabeth said, hugging his arm again.

Beau nodded once again and then stepped back forcing Elizabeth to let go, Her gaze remained fixed on him.

"Then I'll probably see you around. I'm here for a few days myself. Maybe even until Christmas," he said.

"Isn't it weird to think of Christmas when it's

so warm outside? There's snow predicted for New York all this week. I'm so glad to be here," Elizabeth said with a wide smile. "Let's meet for dinner one night?"

"I'll call you. You're staying here at the Royal?" She nodded.

"Jason, we'll have to have that drink one night as well."

Beau nodded to them both and turned back to the lobby. He walked over to the empty concierge desk, noting the sign that it was closed for thirty minutes. Was she taking a break?

Stopping by the registration desk, he asked how he could contact Shelly.

"Sorry sir, we don't give out that information. You'll have to wait until tomorrow when she's back on duty," the desk clerk said. "Or I can leave a note for her. Are you staying here with us?"

Making a quick decision, Beau pulled out his wallet. "I will be. Do you have any suites available?"

A check on the computer confirmed there were suites available. In no time Beau reserved one for a week. He explained his sailboat was at the marina and he'd be bringing in his clothes later.

The clerk asked again if he could take a message for Shelly, but Beau declined.

He wanted to surprise her–and gauge her reaction. Would she be glad to see him? Did she have any regrets on her new career?

Shelly strode into the hotel lobby the next morning at nine with a spring in her step. Today after work she and some friends would be meeting their arched rivals in volleyball. She knew her team was psyched about the event. They'd won two games recently against the rival hotel crew, but before that they'd had a losing streak. She wanted their winning streak to continue.

She put her small purse in the cubby of the desk, and looked up–right into the dark brown eyes of Beaut Charlmers. For a second she caught her breath. Was he real? He had to be, she'd never imagined him in Florida. At least not at her desk. There'd been plenty of daydreams where he'd wooed her on the beach or along a moonlit path of the sprawling resort grounds.

"Beau?" she asked once she could breath again.

"Hello, Shelly."

The voice was his. The face was his. It was him!

"Whatever are you doing here?" she asked, her smile wide and excited.

"I stopped by to see you," he said.

"Me?"

He nodded once.

"You look good. Better than good. I never saw your hair down before. It was always tied back or elegantly done up for a formal event. Guess you got what you wanted in this job. Are you wearing flip flops?"

She gave a short laugh.

"No, but sandals are the next best thing."

She stuck one foot out so he could see the rhinestone-studded white sandals.

He nodded and met her gaze.

"The dress you're wearing is nothing like the tailored business suits I'm used to seeing you in."

She nodded. "Much more comfortable."

Suddenly she felt shy. The strapless sarongs she'd taken to wearing added to the relaxed vacation vibe the hotel wanted, plus they were super comfortable. But that was before Beau skimmed his gaze over her bare shoulders and her breasts which were snugly encased in the bright colorful material.

"I thought I'd never see you again," she said.

Was the breathless voice hers? She cleared her throat.

"I'm guessing you sailed into town."

"The boat's at the marina, I'm staying here."

"Here?"

"I told you, I stopped by to see you. I've been cruising the Caribbean the last few months and this is another island to explore. By now you should be an expert on advising visitors what to see. Maybe you'd give me an island tour." He played down the real reason he was here. Time enough to get to that.

"I'd love to. Not today, of course, I'm working. But I have three days off starting tomorrow. We can see most of the island in that time."

"How about after work today?" he asked.

"Oh, I'm sorry. I can't today. I'm in a volleyball tournament. When the game's over we'll be going to dinner together–hopefully to celebrate another win."

For a split second she considered cutting out of the game, but she couldn't do that to her teammates. Seeing Beau had her thoughts skittering around. Her heart rate sped up and she could feel the heat rise in her cheeks. How often had she thought about him over this last year? She'd never expected him to show up in Key West.

"Is the game on the beach in front of the hotel?" he asked casually.

"No, it's in front of another hotel, about a mile down the beach."

Was he planning to watch? She felt a flutter in her stomach, shyness took hold. Suddenly she felt like a teenager who had attracted the attention of the star quarterback. Whoa—where did that come from? She'd worked with this man for nine years. He was merely greeting a former employee. Nothing had changed in their relationship.

Yeah, but before she'd felt armored in her business suits and professional demeanor.

The volley ball game was played in bikinis with a lot of bare skin showing.

She was very conscious of Beau's reputation as a player in New York. Was he still the darling of the billionaire set even if he was sailing the seven seas? Could she show him the island and then say goodbye again. Another few days to hold her over to when? Forever this time?

What a bittersweet time this would be. She'd do her best to treasurer every minute of their time together.

3

Shelly had trouble concentrating on work after Beau left. Every thought revolved around him and his unexpected arrival.

She was dying to find out what he'd been doing since she last saw him. She wondered if he found the solitary life of sailing his boat fulfilling. He'd been so active in New York. How could he turn that off and be satisfied sailing far from friends and familiar sights?

Hotel guests stopped by seeking ideas on how to spend their days when lying on the beach lost its appeal. Busy executives, social wives and bored teenagers looked for more excitement than watching breakers roll.

Shelly had explored Key West in the first few weeks she'd been a resident and delighted in matching guests with the perfect activity, whether it be parasailing or browsing the quaint shops on Duval Street. For the more adventuresome, there were the Dry Tortugas or reef diving or deep sea sport fishing.

Today, however, she couldn't muster her usual enthusiasm because her thoughts kept returning to Beau.

He'd looked amazing. Tanned and fit. The T-shirt he'd worn displayed impressive muscles. His hair was a bit longer than in Manhattan, but suited a casual retired look.

She checked the guest registry during a lull. He had booked a suite on the top floor.

Why stay here?

Was he tired of the boating scene?

Or did he stay in hotels at all his island explorations?

She had a thousand questions. Impatient with the way the day was dragging, she tried to maintain focus on her job, but thoughts kept returning to Beau.

Finally the workday ended.

She changed into her bathing suit and put her sarong back on until she reached the game site.

Once on the sand, she jogged down to the volleyball setup. Others were already there, but not everyone. She checked her watch. They still had ten minutes before the agreed upon start time.

She dumped her dress and sandals into her tote

and added it to the pile from the others and moved out onto the sand to get some practice in. She'd joined this team last spring and they'd be able to play almost every week except when hurricane Minerva had invaded.

"Hi Shelly," several people called.

She returned greetings and went to stand in a vacant spot.

Concentrating on her game, she was glad for the chance to warm up. The only prize the winners won was bragging rights, but they all played as if they were trying for Olympic gold.

Soon they were playing in earnest. An assist. A slam over the net. A missed return. The game was fast.

"Yours, Shelly," Annabelle, her teammate on the right called.

Shelly looked for the ball, her eye caught by Beau standing on the sidelines, arms crossed, watching her.

The ball bounced right on her head.

Arrrgghh, she'd blown it big time.

With an apologetic look to Annabelle, she tossed the ball back. Every inch of her was attuned to Beau standing on the sidelines. She needed to be all in for the game, but snuck another quick glance to the right.

He was standing there big as life with a wide grin on his face. She'd just done a really dumb non-assist and he was probably laughing up a storm.

Focus!

Doing her best to ignore her awareness that seem to expand exponentially, she concentrated on the game. She did her best but felt self conscious like never before. Why could one person make such a difference?

Bragging rights retained! Shelly joined in the celebration with her teammates, still feeling foolish about her mistake earlier, but happy it hadn't cost them the game.

"Dinner at McDuff's?" someone called.

The agreement was unanimous. McDuff's was a local hole-in-the-wall with beach front setting and picnic tables and benches on the sand. The primary advantage was it was a short walk from the volleyball field. Soon everyone was headed that way.

Shelly looked around for Beau, but didn't see him. Disappointed, she kept a bright smile on her face. She didn't want teammates questioning her.

Ordering the shrimp po'boy, Shelly tried to join in the conversation that swirled around her table. But she couldn't help sneaking glances around in case Beau had followed the group.

"Looking for someone, Shelly?" Annabelle asked, catching her glance over her shoulder.

"No, just seeing who all is here. Sorry about my fumble earlier."

"Yeah, what was up with that? You're one of the best on our team, why the miss?"

"I got distracted."

"With that hunk that watched us for a while?" Marcy asked from across the table. "Did you see him, Annabelle? Tall, dark and hot, hot, hot. I was almost mesmerized."

Shelly shrugged. She was not going to foster speculation. Even though she agreed with Marcy. Beau was hot, hot, hot.

Annabelle said, "There're always people watching. I think we should think about getting some seating, maybe cheapo plastic chairs. We might draw more of an audience if they could sit for the game."

"Nah, we move the location too often. Anyway, they're always tourists, here today, then gone," Marcy said. "And if they don't want to stand, they can sit on the sand."

That was true, Shelly thought. Beau could be leaving the day after tomorrow for all she knew. If so, she'd better make the most of their day tomorrow.

She's missed him so much when she'd first arrived in Key West. For nine years she'd seen him almost every work day and plenty of weekends. They'd worked together flawlessly. She'd admired him so much. Starting his first company while still in college, he'd grown more than one business before turning it over to someone else as he started another one.

He'd seemed driven. Which is why she was so surprised when he turned his back on it all to go sailing.

Over the year her infatuation with her boss had diminished. If asked, she would have said she was over him entirely until he walked up to her desk that morning.

"I'm heading home," Shelly said, scrunching her napkin up and rising to toss the remnants of her sandwich.

She wanted some time alone to think about what she'd say to Beau in the morning. Could she be subtle in posing all her questions? Or just come across as totally nosy?

"Good game. See you after Christmas," Marcy said.

Others at their table called goodbye and Shelly headed for her small cottage.

Twilight had descended a while ago—while the

game was finishing up. It was dark but street lights illuminated the sidewalk enough to walk safely. She took a deep breath smelling the fragrance of some flowers still blooming in the warm humid air even though Christmas was only days away.

Tomorrow she'd see Beau again. Her heart skipped a beat just thinking about him. She'd soak up his very presence to tide her over–until when? Would he ever be back to Key West?

She needed to get over him once and for all. How could she move forward still holding a crush on her former boss?

Concentrating on trying to envision all the women he'd dated while she worked for him, she could remember most. The pretty faces with his in the newspapers. That one spread in People magazine. His taste in women was legendary–blond and beautiful, rich and sophisticated, playgirls to his playboy.

Instead, she remembered the times he'd asked her to play hostess at his Hampton house when holding a party for the company's most favored stockholders. And the times she'd gone as his plus one on several different social events. Not that they were the high society events with dozens of paparazzi, but personal celebrations that he attended without the gossip columnists speculating on who his date was.

Letting herself into her cottage a short time later, she headed for a shower. She was gritty with sand, tired, but not sleepy. After her shower, she'd fix some hot cocoa and pretend it was snowing outside.

When Shelly fixed her hot cocoa she took it into the living room and sat on the sofa. It was still warm enough to have the windows and doors open, but she loved hot cocoa and took a sip.

Glancing around she wondered if she should have decorated her home for Christmas. She hadn't last year—it didn't seem worth it for one person. Plus she was rarely home. Now it looked a little bare.

It wasn't too late. She'd have to think about it.

4

Beau stood at the window of his hotel room gazing out. The sea beyond was dark, but the fairy lights scattered around the resort's grounds illuminated the area in a most inviting way. Pathways were outlined by lamps that added to the romantic ambiance of the place.

He watched as palm trees swayed gently in the breeze and wondered how Shelly liked her new life. It looked totally different from what he knew about her in New York. Was she tired of the constant hot weather? Did she find her job less exciting than her position with him?

He hoped when they got together she'd give him some insight.

He'd come on a mission. He needed to scope out the situation before making his move. But for an instant he wondered if he'd succeed.

His phone rang. It was Jason Wilson.

"Beau, it's the end of a long day. Join me for a drink? I'm sitting at the Beachcomber's Bar right on the beach. Lovely night. Elizabeth's gone off with her friends. Want to keep an old man company?"

"Sounds good. I'll be there in a minute."

Beau had always liked Jason. An astute business man they had had several good discussions on various aspects of building a business.

Elizabeth, however, was a different matter. If she was elsewhere, he'd enjoy talking with someone from the past. That young woman reminded him of a shark always looking for prey. He couldn't believe she hadn't gotten married–it seemed to be her raison d'etre to find a husband. Preferably a rich one.

Beau was always careful when around women like that. He knew his money was a draw. That had never crossed his mind when he set out to become wealthy. A poor childhood had him vow to never live like that again if he could help it.

But once an estimate of his wealth began to circulate, he suddenly had people wanting friendship or more. Not for himself but for either what he could do for them or to latch on and ride the wave of wealth.

It was not something he liked thinking about, but it was his reality.

A short walk along one of the resort's paths and he saw the bar. Jason sat at a small table on the outskirts of the lighted area. The soft sound of small waves washing on shore lent a soothing almost magical mood to the place.

A few other tables were occupied with couples leaning in close as if in intimate conversations.

"Beau, thanks for joining me," Jason smiled.

"Too early for bed, too late to do much. It's good to see you. Let me get a drink and I'll join you."

In less than five minutes he pulled out a chair and sat at the small table. The sand beneath them held onto the warmth of the day contrasting to the cool breeze that came from the sea.

"To living the dream," Jason said raising his glass.

"To living the dream," Beau echoed as he touched the rim of his to Jason's. "And are you living the dream?"

"Not yet. Not like you. I want to hear how you turned your back on everything and set sail for new adventures. Gutsy move if you ask me," Jason said.

"Timing. I'm in my prime. If ever I want to do this, I need to do it when I'm fit, not put it off until I'm too old," Beau said. "I haven't really turned my back on everything. I have a satellite phone, wifi at ports to keep me in touch. But Lyle is doing a great job. I may just sell him the business."

"That's been your secret all along, hasn't it—

bring someone along as you grow a business and then sell out to them. Do you get bored once you've built an empire."

Beau smiled. "Hardly an empire. A successful company here and there. I'm not bored with them as much as the challenge is diminished once it's running successfully. I think I like the risk of failure as something tangible to overcome. You could do it. You're doing well, turn over the day to day operations and go live your dream."

"I don't have the passion in anything these days," Jason said, studying the remaining liquid in his glass. "I'm divorced. Elizabeth is still single and is high maintenance. I'm not as young as you, but still have some good years ahead. I'm just not sure I can leave the safety of work to step into the unknown."

"You'll never know unless you try."

"So tell me about that. Talk about total change. From your home in the Hamptons to a sailboat? Quite a change."

Beau started to share his experiences since leaving New York when Elizabeth showed up.

She looked beautiful. She wore a sparkling silver dress which displayed her figure to perfection. She had a filmy wrap covering her arms.

"So this is where I find you. And Beau. Lovely evening isn't it?"

Both men rose as she reached the table. Jason reached out to get a chair from a nearby table for his daughter.

"Party ended early?" he asked as she smiled at him and Beau.

"Several of the women are going scuba diving tomorrow and so had to stop drinking so many hours before. The rest of us decided to call it a night. Now I'm glad I did," she said smiling brightly at Beau. "Have you two been here for long?"

"Not too long. Can I get you a drink?" Beau asked.

"G&T. Thanks."

Beau went to the bar, turning to look at the Wilsons while the bartender prepared the gin and tonic. He became immediately suspicious about Elizabeth's arrival. How had she known to come to this bar to find her father? A glance at his watch allayed his suspicions somewhat. It was almost midnight and he knew diving was never recommended if a person had a hangover.

He'd finish his drink and call it a night. He hadn't arranged a time to meet with Shelly in the morning but planned to be near the concierge desk by nine—the time it open.

"I was telling Dad that there's going to be a kind of crab bake on the beach tomorrow evening for the wedding party and guests. Will you join us? It starts around 6 and goes on until who knows," Elizabeth said after she thanked him for her drink.

"I have other plans, but thanks. It sounds like fun."

"What kind of plans?" she asked.

Beau wanted to tell her it was none of her business, but merely said he was meeting an old friend and spending the day together.

"Well the invitation is open. Come if you can even if later."

He inclined his head, but carefully refrained from giving any hint he might accept.

"Beau was telling me about his life these days. Maybe I should retire and try something different," Jason said slowly.

"Like what?" Elizabeth asked staring at her father in some surprise.

"That's the problem, no idea."

"While I think it's wonderful for a young man like Beau to do that, you'd be bored to tears in no time," Elizabeth said.

Beau swallowed the last of his drink and set the glass down on the table.

"Good to see you both. I'm heading for bed now. I'm meeting my friend early."

Despite their protests, he rose and swiftly followed the meandering path back to the hotel.

When he reached his room he found a message waiting. Shelly had called to say she'd meet him in the lobby at seven o'clock and not to eat breakfast because she knew the best place on the island.

As he got ready for bed, he considered the difference between Elizabeth and Shelly. He'd take Shelly every time.

5

Shelly leaned against the concierge desk checking her watch once again. It was still five minutes until seven. She tried to be patient, it wasn't even the time she said to meet, but she wanted to hurry so they'd see the sunrise.

When the elevator dinged again she looked over and saw Beau step out. She smiled and hurried to meet him.

"Good morning," she said brightly.

"Good morning, I take it there's a reason to meet so early," Beau said.

"Yes, but we have to hurry. There's this little restaurant right on the beach that has a beautiful view of the sunrise, which is due in just a few minutes. I think we can make it."

She hurried out of the hotel with Beau keeping pace with her. She'd discovered the little café her first week on the island and made it a point to visit frequently always adjusting the time for sunrise each day.

They walked briskly along the sidewalk heading east.

"No car?" he asked.

She smiled.

"No car. I didn't have one in New York, so wanted to see if I could get by without one here. And I can. I have a bike that I use if I need to get somewhere quickly, but otherwise, I don't live far from the hotel. So I walk everywhere or take my bike."

"Even in the rain?"

"A little water never hurt anyone. I do have a raincoat. Here we are."

She turned onto a pathway that led to Marty's Café. Sitting at one of the empty tables right next to the sandy beach, she smiled at Beau.

"Now watch, the sun will be rising in just another minute or two."

He sat facing east studying the colorful dots of high clouds sprinkled across the sky. The pink was fading into white. Slowly the orange ball began its ascent until it cleared the horizon.

She turned from the view back to him.

"Beautiful, isn't it? Though I expect you see a lot of sunrises on your boat. And sunsets."

He nodded and turned his chair slightly.

"It never gets old, though, does it?" he asked.

"What can I get you?" The waitress placed two glasses of water on the table. "Coffee?"

"Yes, please. And we'd like your Key West Special Breakfast," Shelly said, looking at Beau for confirmation.

He nodded.

When the waitress went back inside the small café, he asked what the special was.

"Just the best eggs and fixin's you'll ever eat. And it's big. I figured you could use a full breakfast before our sightseeing adventure."

Beau smiled slightly. "Sightseeing adventure?"

"Don't you think that sounds more fun than merely sightseeing around the island?"

"An adventure is always more fun," he agreed.

"So tell me about sailing the seven seas. Is it all you thought it would be?"

He was quiet for a moment, then said, "In some ways it's more than I expected and in others not what I was envisioning at all. For one thing, I didn't realize how long it would take to get use to the solitude."

Shelly nodded. "I expect that felt totally different. Was it hard to kick back and do nothing? I remember we were on the go from early to late so many days and you more than me."

"It was different I'll say that. Which gave me

plenty of time to think about what the future might hold. And to learn patience to fish. Many of my dinners include fresh caught fish."

The waitress arrived with two platters full. The eggs were scrambled with cheese, the rashers of bacon were crisp, the spicy sausage links browned to perfection. There were grits on the side and toast and jam.

"Thanks," Shelly said as the waitress turned to leave.

"This looks great. One of the things I like about visiting different ports is not having to cook for myself," Beau said as they began to eat.

For a few moments, neither spoke. As the meal was consumed, conversation slowly resumed.

"Tell me about Key West and your life here. From what I've seen so far, it's completely different from what we had in New York. Is it all you expected?" he asked.

She nodded. "And more. I never thought I'd become a member of a volleyball team. I'm also now certified as a SCUBA diver and love diving in the clear water around here and seeing all the colorful tropical fish. My job is such I don't take it home or spend more than the seven hours required at the hotel. That's the biggest difference," she said with a teasing grin.

He acknowledged the reference to their working habits. Many nights they'd stayed at the office late or took work home.

"I have my SCUBA certificate but don't get in many dives. First the Atlantic is cold up in New England. And I don't dive alone, so have to connect with other divers which has proved few and far between."

"So we can go one day if you like. I have a friend who has a boat we can use."

"I have a boat we can use," he said.

She laughed. "I forgot. That'd be great. I think tomorrow's supposed to be nice weather wise."

"It's a date," Beau said as he finished his coffee.

Shelly felt her heart flutter a little at his words.

Imagine a date with Beau Charlmers. Like that would ever happen.

"Do you miss Farmington?" she asked.

"Sometimes. I've called Lyle two or three times over the year. He's doing a fine job. I've proposed he buy me out and he's thinking about it."

"If he does, you'll have to start another company won't you?" she asked. "Isn't that how you operate?"

"Things change. I'm considering something else now. We'll see. Want to take a walk along the beach? That's something I haven't done–walked with a pretty woman on the shore."

Shelly blinked. That was totally unexpected. Beau had never complimented her before.

"I'd love to. We can walk back to the resort that way. It's sugar-sand all the way. And if you haven't explored the resort grounds, you'll love them. There are several areas where one can just sit and enjoy the view and the sound of the water. And on the beach there're lounge chairs, umbrellas and a bar."

"Does the hotel permit employees to take advantage of the amenities?"

"I don't think so, but I've never tried so who knows."

They kicked off their shoes when they stepped off the deck of the café and onto the sand. Walking to the water's edge, they turned toward the resort.

After a few minutes of silence, Beau asked,

"Are you seeing someone these days?"

Shelly was surprised again. This Beau wasn't the man she remembered. He'd never have asked that question.

"No. I have a bunch of friends, but no one special. How about you?"

If he could ask, so could she. They weren't boss/PA any more.

What were they?

Acquaintances? Colleague? Friends?

"Hard to start much less continue a relationship from a sailboat."

"You dated a lot in New York, none of those women kept in touch?"

"There's one at the resort right now, actually. I remember taking her out a few times, but now I'm wondering why. My perspective seems to have changed."

Shelly laughed.

"Things look different now, once we pull away from what everyone else is doing and live on our terms. I can't imagine going back to a business suit and high heels. I think I've found my sweet spot and never plan to leave."

"Never say never—you don't know what might arise."

"True, but it'd have to be something extraordinarily amazing to lure me away from Key West."

6

The water was warm as they waded through the spent waves. Shelly wasn't sure what to suggest as a sightseeing guide. Most of the tourists staying at the hotel wanted to see Hemingway's house, some opted for the lighthouse or southern most point. Others wanted the deep sea experience diving or sport fishing. The options seemed so mundane now. What would Beau really like?

When they reached the resort, the path from the beach led beside one of the outdoor dining patios. Where the sand met the concrete walkway there was a low faucet to rinse the sand off feet. Beau offered his hand to Shelly to use as balance as she rinsed off one foot and put her sandal back on, then the other foot.

"I'll return the favor," she said, still holding onto Beau's hand while he rinsed his feet.

"Beau!" A voice called from the dining patio. "Beau!"

He glanced over and saw Elizabeth rising from

a table of four with three other women.

Shelly turned and watched as Elizabeth made her way through the tables to reach the edge a few feet from them.

"Good morning. You're out and about early. Want to join us for coffee?" she said with a bright smile.

Beau kept hold of Shelly's hand and pulled her closer to him.

"Not this morning, thanks. Shelly and I have plans."

Elizabeth's smiled slipped a little at she glanced at Shelly.

"Hi. You look familiar. Have we met?"

"At the mayor's ball two years ago," Shelly replied evenly.

Elizabeth looked as if she was trying to remember, but then shrugged and turned back to Beau.

"Maybe we can get together this evening. Give me a call," she said.

She waited a minute as if expecting a response from him, but Beau merely inclined his head slightly.

Slowly Elizabeth returned to her table. She was immediately peppered with questions from the other women.

"That's Elizabeth Wilson, isn't it?" Shelly asked as they began walking toward the front of the resort.

She glanced at their linked hands. Beau must have forgotten he was holding her hand as he hadn't let go.

Resisting temptation to check out Elizabeth to see if she noticed they were still holding hands, she let hers tighten slightly in his.

"She and her father are here for a wedding," he said succinctly.

"Key West is a favorite destination for weddings," she murmured.

She herself would love to be married on the beach at sunset, that is if she ever found a man she could love who'd love her.

"Our tour begins now, we'll wander over to Duval Street, the main drag, and you can check out the southern architecture and the gazillion shops and bars. It's said you can buy anything money can afford on Duval Street," she said as they reached the sidewalk in front of the resort.

Before long they were wandering along the busy sidewalk, dodging tourists and locals alike.

They perused the window display at a jewelry store. Refused to be lured into a T-shirt establishment by a zealous vendor. Crossed the street for a closer look at a real estate office with pictures of homes for sale in their window.

"Prices are comparable to New York," he commented as they discussed the various properties.

"But the houses are cuter. I love all the pastels instead of so much brick. I'm buying a little cottage. It's small, but darling."

"I'd like to see it."

"Sure. We can have dinner tonight there unless you have other plans."

"I thought we'd dine out. You are spending the day showing me the sights."

"Yes, but we'll be tired and it'll be more relaxing at my place."

"I look forward to it," he said with a grin.

They wandered into an art gallery with an eclectic display of paintings and sculptures. Ranging from typical surf scenes to modern art, the prices reflected the high value for each item.

"I don't guess you have a lot of room on a sailboat for art," she said as she studied one painting of a hidden garden.

"No." He looked around.

"You had some lovely ones in your home in the Hamptons," she said as they moved on.

"I didn't pick them out, the interior designer did."

"So what do you like?" she asked.

"I prefer paintings that look like I'm looking out a window at a particular scene—like that one of the garden."

"I like that, too. And the one here," she said pointing to another. "My folks decorated our family home mostly with photographs. We have tons of posed family groups shots and candid pictures from their early marriage days to last Christmas. None of us is big into art, I guess. Did your family go in for art?"

He looked at her for a long moment.

"I think I can safely say my mom went in for original art pieces. Meaning she hung crayon drawings I did all over the place. We couldn't afford to buy pictures so mine were everywhere. I'm not an artist, but my Mom loved my pictures."

Shelly nodded. "I know what you mean, my folks still have one of my early finger paintings on the fridge. And some from my brother and sister. I'm in my thirties now when do you suppose they'll take them down?"

"Maybe never."

"How long did your mom keep yours up?" she asked.

"Until the day she died," he replied, turning to study some of the other paintings.

She reached out and touched his arm.

"I'm sorry if I brought up sad memories."

He looked at her.

"She died almost twenty years ago. I had to pack everything up and move out of our apartment almost immediately."

"Did you keep the pictures?" she asked.

He nodded, then gave a deprecating sound. "Somewhere in the storage unit I kept is an old cardboard box of things she cherished. My pictures included."

"That's sweet. Maybe you should display them."

"It wouldn't go with the decor on a sailboat."

"But it would mean a lot to you to remember her by displaying some things, wouldn't it? You can hang drawings on your tiny fridge."

He gazed down into her eyes for a long moment.

Shelly wondered if he was going to speak when he broke eye contact and turned away.

"You still have room for mementos from your childhood in your boat. Otherwise it's not a home."

"And the difference between a boat and a home?" he asked.

"A home is special. You're safe, it's as if the place wraps its arms around you and welcomes you back with love. You can totally be yourself," she said.

Beau moved to a small painting of a cottage by the sea, with flowers spilling all over the garden.

"This looks like a home," he said slowly.

Shelly studied the painting.

"It does. Looking at it makes me feel happy. I bet it's a happy place, too. The gardens speak of personal love, the curtains on the windows are light and probably move in any breeze. I love it."

She stepped closer to read the card affixed to the wall beside the painting. "A Rosemary Collins painted it. I wonder if she has other paintings here."

"We can ask," Beau said.

It turned out there were three other Rosemary Collins paintings, all of the same subject but at different times of day or seasons.

"Oh, I really love this one," Shelly said as they viewed the Christmas painting. The small cottage had been decorated for Christmas with the window displaying a Christmas tree.

"I'll buy it for you," Beau said.

"No, thanks," she replied still studying the picture.

"Why not, if you like it. You're taking time from your own day to show me around. It's the least I can do."

She turned to him exasperated.

"Let me explain something to you. People do things for the joy of doing them, not because they expect some kind of payment for doing it."

He narrowed his gaze.

"I am happy to see you again. I thought for sure our goodbyes in New York would be the last time I saw you. Happily, I was wrong. So I'm having a great time showing off my new home to someone who hasn't seen it before. I do not need any kind of reimbursement for that."

He reached out and brushed a strand of hair from her cheek.

"If you're sure."

"I am. So thank you for thinking of it, but definitely no. Now, let's see the rest of the exhibit and be on our way."

"Next stop?" he asked.

"We'll have lunch at a great place I know and then get bikes and ride to the southern most point of the Continental U.S. A must-not-miss-stop on our tour of Key West."

Shelly tried to focus on the paintings they were looking at as they ambled around the room, but her cheek still tingled from Beau's touch. He'd rarely ever touched her when they worked together. An occasional taking her arm or touch on the back if guiding her into a formal event.

It was nothing. Inconsequential. Ignore it.

He made a comment about a painting. She tried to formulate a response, but it was easier said than done. Suddenly she wanted to get back outside, take the walk to the sea food shack she knew had the best po'boy sandwiches on the island.

"I'm getting sensory overload," she said. "They're all starting to blur to me."

"Then let's leave."

When they stepped outside, Beau noted the address of the building.

"Thinking of coming back?" Shelly asked.

"I might. If I could find a spot on the boat for a picture."

"Isn't your boat fully decorated?" she asked as they strolled along the sidewalk.

"I'm not sure you'd call it decorated. It is as it came. Clean and tidy. Serviceable, functional."

"Home?"

"Before your clarification earlier I might have said yes, now I'm not so sure. Maybe I've just not taken time to feel it wrap its arms around me," he said in a teasing tone.

She laughed.

"Okay, home might feel differently to different people. Can I see your boat?"

"Sure. We can go sailing tomorrow if you like. Even do some diving. With two of us it'd be safe."

"That sounds like a great plan."

Another day with Beau. How cool was that? She'd take whatever time she could get. Who knew if he'd ever be back to Key West?

They rented two bicycles at a local shop. Even though Shelly had her own bike, she didn't want to take the time to go home to get it.

They pedaled lazily through the streets, enjoying the pastel colored homes and profuse gardens spilling over with blossoms despite the fact it was almost Christmas.

Shelly loved this part of old Key West. The never ending summer delighted her and she hoped she'd always appreciate it and not take it for granted.

"This is it?" Beau asked when they came to a stop near the buoy declaring the spot the southern most point in the continental U.S. There was a line of people waiting to take pictures with the landmark.

"A bit anti-climatic I think," she said. "Do you want your picture taken beside it?"

"I'll pass. Now I've seen it. Is there some special rite of passage or something?"

"Not that I know of. Just a tourist spot. I don't know if Alaska has a similar most northern point of the North American continent," she said.

"It's probably in Canada anyway. Wherever it is, I can't see people lining up like this."

"This isn't bad. Wait until you see Mallory Square."

"The sunset place?" he asked.

"Yes, another must see. We can take a tour of Hemingway's house, then a leisurely ride back, turn in the bikes and head for the docks. It gets really crowded the closer to sunset, but until then there are things to see. It'll be fun. At least once."

"I never saw myself as a typical tourist."

"Live a little like the majority of us. We all can't be gazillionaires."

He nodded as they turned their bikes and headed back to the center of town to turn them back in.

7

By the time they reached Shelly's house it was full dark. They'd joined in the nightly celebration of the sunset at Mallory Square. Watching the mimes, exploring the little kiosks, and cheering when the sun set was all part of the fun in the crowd at the pier. Once twilight began to fall they left for her cottage. She hadn't left on a light so fumbled a minute to get the door open.

"Sorry you couldn't see the place in the daytime. It's really cute, I think. Come in."

Beau stepped inside and glanced around. The set up was as far from his designer's decorated house as possible. Mostly he noticed color every where. One wall was a deep turquoise, another a very pale hue of the same color. Her sofa was yellow, what he could see with all the pillows piled high in every shade imaginable.

She had wicker furniture, a sturdy dining table and four chair. The place mats on the table were a riot of color. Fresh flowers sat in the bowl in the center.

There were big windows which reflected the interior lights now but would give the feeling of almost being outdoors when the sun shone. Pictures decorated the walls, some of family, others of scenic sights.

"I thought we could have stir fry for dinner," she said as she went into the kitchen. It was a separate room with a wide door.

"I'll put the rice on and get busy with the vegetables and meat," she called.

"Sounds good."

He wandered to some of the photographs, smiling when he recognized Shelly as a young girl in family pictures with her parents, siblings. And a couple with some other girls he didn't know.

"Do you want something to drink until dinner's ready?" she called.

"No, I'm fine."

Standing at the kitchen entrance he leaned against the doorway watching her as she chopped the vegetables and chicken for the stir fry.

"Do you like to cook?" he asked.

"It's not my passion. And I eat out a lot–a carry over from my days in New York when I was too tired at night to cook. It was habit that I usually picked something up on the way home. Unless it was a night we ordered in at the office."

He nodded. "Do you miss it? New York?"

She tilted her head slightly as if considering.

"Not really. I miss some of my friends. We keep in touch by phone, but once you're not a daily part of life, it's easy to slip away. I've made new friends here."

"Right, you love it here and will never leave."

She laughed her eyes meeting his.

"Right. Tell me what you miss about New York."

"Like the crowds, the traffic, the winters?" he asked.

"That doesn't sound like much to miss," she said as she pulled a wok out from a lower cabinet.

"I missed you," Beau said softly.

"What?" Shelly stopped mid move and stared at him. "Me?" she squeaked.

"We worked closely together for nine years. Of course I missed you."

"Oh, to handle your phone calls, which are probably non-existent on a boat."

"To bounce ideas off of. To get your opinion on things. To hear you argue passionately against something I strongly supported."

She carefully placed the wok on the stove.

"Like the Fleming account."

"Ouch, that would be the one you remember. Lucky fluke that you were right."

"There were one or two other times," she pointed out.

"True, but do you know you were practically the only one at the end who wasn't a yes person. Even Lyle didn't stand up for anything he wanted if I wasn't already on board with it."

"You were the boss, I think employees were afraid to rock the boat."

"You weren't."

She shrugged. "I guess I felt if you asked my opinion you wanted it for good or bad or you wouldn't have asked."

"True." He glanced over his shoulder. "I'm surprised you don't have any Christmas decorations up."

"I'm enjoying the ones at the hotel. It seemed silly for me to get a tree, decorate it myself and then take it down by myself. I think that's a tradition for families or if you plan to entertain, which I don't. I remember the beautiful trees at your home when you held the Christmas parties."

"Another decorator's delight," he murmured.

"So what was Christmas like when you were a boy?" she asked, dumping in the vegetables and meat in the hot oil. Taking a pair of chopsticks, she stirred.

He didn't answer for a moment until Shelly looked at him.

"Nothing elaborate. I remember making strings of popcorn and paper chains. My mom had a few decorations, not many, but enough with our homemade efforts that the tree always looked special. I don't remember lights when I was really young. But by the time I was a teenager we had strings of lights. Which got tangled every year and it was my job to untangle them."

Shelly smiled and nodded.

"I know. I'm lucky, I never had the untangle-the-lights job at home. Either my dad or one of my brothers did that. I loved putting on the tinsel. My mom was so persnickety about that. We had to do one strand at a time."

"That had to take patience."

"Yeah, which we didn't have much of as kids. We'd all wait until she left the room and then threw bunches on the back. Of course she knew that but never said a word."

"You're not going home for Christmas?"

"No. Staying here. I went home last year. My parents are coming to visit in January."

"Plans for Christmas Day?"

"Not really. A couple of married friends have invited me to share dinner with their family, but I haven't said yes yet. I might want to spend the day by myself."

"Spend it with me," Beau said. "We'll get a tree, decorate it and I can have the hotel do up a dinner for us."

She turned off the stove and turned to face him.

"I'd love to spend Christmas with you. I didn't think you'd be here that long, it's still a few days away."

"I'm not on any deadline. I can stay as long as I choose."

"Then yes, sure, fine. Sounds like a plan."

Shelly served their plates and carried them to the dining table. Getting silverware she set the table quickly and brought iced water in a pitcher.

"This is delicious," Beau said a few bites into the stir fry.

"I'm glad you like it. Of all the places you could have eaten tonight, this is hardly the best."

"The food's good and so's the company."

"I have Key Lime Pie for dessert," she blurted out, flustered by his compliment. This was not the boss she remembered. He was always so focused on work he never had time for small talk or compliments.

"Did you make that, too?" he asked.

"Last night. On the chance you might stop by."

Oh great, now she revealed she was hoping he'd stop by.

"I look forward to that next. Tell me more about your job here. It can't be as challenging as the work we did."

"It's challenging in trying to find the perfect activity or adventure for people staying in the resort. Experiences that they'll love, remember and rave about. Sometimes I hit it out of the park so to speak. Other times I haven't a clue because I get no feedback. I spent as much time as I could when I first got here in trying everything I could so I can recommend from experience."

"Dealing with the public constantly has to be difficult."

"Some days it can be. But as I said before, once I leave the hotel, I have no further work to do until I show up the next morning."

"While when working together you often took home work, even if we stayed until after nine."

"True, but it was exciting work. Challenging as you said. Now that I've experienced a more relaxed kind of job, I think of it as my next stage. My New York years made me a good match for this one. And I appreciate my free time even more. You must as well, living on a sailboat and going wherever the mood strikes."

"For the most part."

After dinner, Shelly suggested they take their pie and coffee to her small patio. She had a couple of Adirondack chairs and tables near the house. The evening was pleasant with a slight breeze. The light spilling from the side windows was all the illumination they needed. The flowers blooming around the perimeter of the yard filled the air with sweet fragrance.

"You have a nice place here," Beau said as he settled in.

"I like it. I spend a lot of time outside. My apartment in New York didn't even have a balcony. I really like the flowers and gardening—at least as much as I do."

She finished her pie and put the plate on the table between them. Beau followed a moment later.

"Do you ever wish you could go back and change something and then imagine how that would change your life?" she asked, leaning back and gazing up to the star studded sky.

"I'd change my mom's dying if I could."

"That must have been so hard. You haven't mentioned your father. Is he not in the picture?"

He was quiet for a moment, then said, "My

folks weren't married. He died in the first Gulf War so my mom said. I never knew him. They had split before I was old enough to remember him. It was always just my mom and me."

"No grandparents, aunts or uncles or cousins?" Shelly asked, trying to imagine being without any relatives when she'd grown up surrounded by lots of family.

"None."

"So how did you manage?"

"Being alone and broke is a huge motivator. I was determined to make it big no matter what. Some of it was anger at life, some gut reaction to having nothing at one time. It also guarantees taking risks that most men won't. If you have nothing, or come from nothing, you'll know no matter what happens you can take care of yourself. I think people who grow up with certain prosperity are more risk adverse."

"Maybe," she murmured trying to imagine her friends being dedicated to making it big and couldn't.

She had a million more questions she wanted to ask, but refrained. Today had been surreal. Almost like old friends, yet not. She'd just learned more about his personal life than she'd known in the nine years she'd worked for him.

Would tomorrow bring more revelations? She hoped so.

If nothing else, they'd spend the day sailing, diving and if they returned in time, they could get that Christmas tree and some decorations and share in that happy task.

8

Getting directions from Shelly, Beau walked back to the resort instead of calling for a taxi. The streets were well lit. Couples and groups walked along the sidewalks still enjoying the evening. It wasn't late though it had been dark for hours.

He thought about the day with Shelly. She constantly surprised him. Some of it had to do with his expectations that she'd be the same efficient personal assistant she'd been before.

Instead she was carefree and happy and shared that with everyone.

She looked fantastic. The slight tan accentuated her blue eyes and blonde hair. The enthusiasm with which she met everything was refreshing. When her hair had been blown about while riding the bikes, she'd just laughed it off and brushed it off her face. She was comfortable with who she was.

The best part, however, was she hadn't pushed for anything.

He knew he was jaded. Over the years since he'd made his first million, more women than he could count purported to be friends. But it was the kind of friendship that included being seen in all the right places, receiving tokens of affection–usually from Tiffany's. And making plans without a thought to what he might want.

Shelly had suggested seeing things she thought he'd enjoy. Her whole day had been to show him her new home and all the best parts.

She'd refused his offer to buy her that picture.

Had invited him for dinner at her place rather than be seen at some fancy restaurant on the island.

She wasn't the same woman he'd expected, but he liked this new version even better.

The question was, could he convince her to see him in a different way? There was a certain reserve between them. A bit relaxed from their roles in the office. Yet not like they were friends.

Though he wasn't sure he'd know friendship if it slapped him in his face.

Devon and he had been friends, back in high school. But they'd drifted apart and lost touch almost twenty years ago. Both loners, both with single moms struggling to make ends meet. Was that the only bond they'd shared?

In the early days of building his first company, he'd thought he'd made friends, but in every case the friendship had been financially driven—what he could do for the other man.

He had enough money to last ten lifetimes. He could buy almost anything he wanted—except genuine friendship. Would he ever come to trust someone or always be on the lookout for ulterior motives?

When he entered the brightly lit lobby of the hotel he did a quick scan looking for either of the Wilson's. He wanted to avoid contact if he could. He almost laughed at the idea. He was fully capable of refusing any invitation from them. He just didn't want the hassle.

When he entered his suite he noticed the message light blinking on the phone. Crossing the sitting room, he lifted it and punched in the numbers to retrieve it.

Two messages from Elizabeth and one from her father. He erased them all. He was here to see Shelly, not renew friendships from New York. Maybe they'd get the hint eventually.

Shelly was already at the dive shop by nine, the time she and Beau had planned to meet.

"Going out with friends?" Dave asked.

He owned the small dive shop on the beach. Not only did he sell and rent scuba equipment, he was the one who kept her tanks filled and in perfect working order.

"A friend. He's done some scuba diving as well, so we're going out for the day. We're meeting here."

"Perfect day for it. No storms in sight, light winds. Where're you going?"

"I haven't a clue."

"Good morning," Beau said behind her as he stepped into the small sales room.

"Hi, good morning," she replied with a big smile. "Beau meet Dave. He's the best scuba instructor on the island."

"I doubt that," Dave said easily holding out his hand to Beau. "But if she wants to keep thinking that, I'm all for it. Shelly tells me you're already SCUBA certified."

"I am and I have equipment on the boat, but my tanks aren't full. Any chance I can rent here to save time?" Beau asked.

"Sure thing. When you bring the tanks back, bring yours and I'll fill them," Dave said. "Let's get you fitted out."

Shelly watched as Dave found the perfect

double tank for Beau. As they talked, Beau asked where the best diving site would be. Soon he and Dave were discussing directions, distances and what could be expected at each location. Dave even pulled out some charts and pointed out several locations. Beau included the charts in the rental.

"Ready?" he asked Shelly.

"Yes."

She picked up her gear and started for the door.

"Have fun," Dave called.

"I have a cab waiting," Beau said as they walked out of the shop. "I didn't want to carry our gear to the boat. Plus I had the hotel make us a picnic basket for lunch and didn't want to carry that around either."

"Sounds like you planned this perfectly," she said with a grin.

Happy in his company, she looked forward to another day together.

When they reached the marina, Beau shouldered his equipment and carried the wicker basket the hotel had prepared containing all the items he'd ordered for lunch.

Shelly carried her gear and followed him down the dock. She looked around at the boats moored in slips along the dock and the larger ones anchored a short distance away. One especially large boat caught her eye.

"How do we get to your boat?" she asked, studying the large yacht.

"Walk to the slip I have it in and step onboard," he said glancing at the yacht in the harbor.

"That isn't mine."

"I figured as much, it isn't a sailboat. But there are some sailboats at anchorage and not tied to the dock."

"First come first serve for the guest slips. My timing was good. Here we are."

Beau turned to the small walkway beside a sleek white sailboat bobbing gently on the waves.

Shelly had been on several different boats since she took up scuba diving, so was an old hand at getting on board, stowing her gear beneath the bench seat.

Beau put his equipment near hers.

"Want a quick tour?" he asked as he headed below with the picnic basket.

"Yes, please," she said with a smile.

It was a standard thirty foot sailboat. Easy enough for a solo sailor to handle. Everything was stowed away neatly. The inside as well as the outside was immaculate. He pointed out the features and then led the way back to the deck.

"Shall I cast off?" she asked as he did his preliminary check before starting the small engine.

"Yes, thanks."

Efficiently casting off and stowing the lines, Shelly gave a half laugh as the day began in earnest.

9

In only moments they were slowly moving out of the marina. Once clear of the breakwater Beau cut the motor and began raising the main sail.

Shelly pitched in and soon the boat began scooting across the waves in total silence.

She sat near him once they were underway and gazed around enjoyed the beautiful day, the warm sun and the calm sea.

"What a perfect day," she said.

Beau nodded. "I'm heading for that spot that Dave recommended, off the beaten track of the tourists but not too far."

"Can you read those charts or do your rely on GPS?" Shelly asked.

"I do my best with the charts and then will cross check sometimes with GPS. I've improved tremendously over the last year."

"Tell me where you've been diving before," she invited.

Beau replied, telling her about learning in the cold waters off Massachusetts and finding how much more he enjoyed it in the Caribbean. He even bought an underwater camera and took some pictures of exotic fish or coral formations that caught his eye.

When they reached the spot Dave recommended, Beau dropped anchor and they prepared to dive.

Shelly couldn't help noticing how fit Beau was when he took off his shirt. He'd worn his beach shorts bathing suit so didn't need to change. He was so tanned and toned, she had a hard time not staring.

Until she felt his eyes on her when she removed her shorts and shirt. Her one-piece suit was best for diving. It clung to every inch of her and she couldn't help being a bit self-conscious at his appreciative look.

Grinning, she faced him.

"Not what we wore in New York. You were hiding behind all those suits."

"And you camouflaged a pretty spectacular body in your suits," he returned, drawing a finger down her bare arm.

Shelly felt the touch ratchet up her heart rate. Swallowing hard, she tried to laugh it off, but the truth was his touch electrified her.

Great, just what she needed—to be even more aware of Beau.

She turned deliberately and began to pull on her tanks, doing her best to breathe.

Checking each other's gear once on, Beau set a marker buoy to let anyone passing know there were divers, then used the diving platform to step into the sea. Shelly followed immediately.

The day was as close to perfect as Shelly ever hoped to have. The water was crystal clear and swarming with colorful tropical fish. They followed one school of bright yellow fish, then were fortunate enough to spot a manatee in the distance. Circling around, she was delighted with all the aquatic life.

Lunch was delicious. The hotel had sent cold fried chicken and a fruit and even included a small chocolate mousse dessert for each. Filling, yet light enough not to interfere with diving later.

In the months since they'd left New York, they'd each kept in touch with different people in the company so brought each other up to date on what they knew.

"I bet it's hard to make friends when you're traveling all the time," Shelly commented as she finished the last of the mousse.

He looked at her.

"It's hard any time these days. I never know if they value me for friendship or for my money."

"Ouch, what a cynical view. Why wouldn't people like you for who you are, not your bank account?"

He shrugged. "Just saying that's been my experience over the years."

"You don't think I'm like that, do you?"

He laughed and looked deep into her eyes.

"Shelly, you're probably the one person on this earth I don't suspect. When we worked together, you stood up to me more times than I care to remember. You are real and honest and I know you don't constantly think about money or being seen in all the right places."

"Good. I would be crushed if you thought I was some sort of gold digger."

"An old-fashioned term."

"Maybe, but it's a perfect description."

She looked at him thoughtfully.

"I think some of the women you dated in New York could be classified like that," she said slowly.

He nodded.

"Make that most. I enjoyed some of them for their company. But there was always something just a little off that I'd get to feeling antsy and stop seeing them."

"Well, you're safe here in Key West. I'm the only one who knows who you are, to Dave and others you're my friend Beau from New York."

"Elizabeth Wilson and her father are staying the hotel, don't forget."

"Oh." She thought about that for a moment. "Is she still single?"

"I'd say so."

"Then watch yourself, I thought she was on the lookout for a rich husband when you were dating her a couple of years ago. That probably hasn't changed."

"Why didn't you warn me?" he asked.

Laughing, she shook her head. "I drew the line at your personal life. How presumptuous that would have been if I'd said anything. I can imagine your expression if I told you that back then."

He nodded, his eyes sparkling. "That would have surprised the heck out of me."

She laughed again. "I'm sure."

"Did you date when you lived in New York?" he asked.

"Of course."

"I never knew that."

"Well, you didn't have to call florists and have flowers sent to me or order stuff from the local jewelry store. I had more knowledge than you did.

And as I recall, I never had a picture in the local papers."

"Any serious?" he asked.

"Not serious enough to stop me from moving to Key West," she said.

"Guess that answers that."

They had one more dive and then headed back to the marina.

"It's been a great day," Shelly said, pleasantly tired. "I'm so glad you wanted to do this."

"I've enjoyed myself. It's been months since I was diving. It's too cold in the northern waters now, and not as much aquatic life to see as here. Up for dinner? Maybe you know a great casual seafood place we could have dinner–my treat tonight. You're too tired to cook."

"No dressing up, huh?"

"I'd like to go just as we are."

She nodded and smiled.

"I do know just the place. It's a favorite with my volley ball team. We may run into some of my friends there."

"I'm up for that if you are."

"I want to go home first however and wash the salt water off. I'll give you the address and we'll meet there in an hour," she said.

"Deal."

They caught a cab from the marina. Shelly was dropped at her cottage and then the cab continued on to the hotel. Beau was going to have the tanks dropped at Dave's in the morning to be refilled.

A bellman jumped forward to carry the diving gear. Beau was half way across the lobby when Elizabeth Wilson popped up right in front of him.

"Hi Beau," she said.

She was dressed up for dinner though he thought it was early for that.

"Elizabeth," he said, stopping so he didn't run her down.

"Care to join us for dinner? Dad will be down soon. We're trying a new restaurant recommended for us. It's supposed to be one of the best on the island."

"I already have dinner plans, but thank you for the invitation."

"How about tomorrow night or the next?" she asked. "You can't be booked up every night. How many people do you know in Key West?"

"Sometimes you only need one. Have a nice evening," he said sidestepping around her and catching up with the bellman waiting patiently by the elevator.

10

Beau arrived at the restaurant before Shelly. He waited near the door watching as people entered. The customers reflected most of what he was seeing in Key West–laid back casual. It was hard to feel rushed in this tropical climate. And hard to think about business when the gentle sea breeze made everything fresh.

"Hi," Shelly said as she walked up to him. "You must have been a million miles away, you didn't see me coming."

He smiled not wanting her to know exactly where his thoughts were.

"This place must do a good business, there have been customers streaming in and so far no one's come out," he said as he held the door for her.

"McDuff's really good and not too expensive. Plus there's a big deck right on the water where most customers congregate."

They were soon seated on the outdoor deck

and orders taken. A couple called out to Shelly and she waved.

"I walked over from the hotel and passed a Christmas tree lot. We can shop there after dinner for your tree," he said.

"Then maybe get one for you, too. We should also stop for some popcorn and construction paper. I don't have any ornaments. My folks started buying each of us kids a special ornament every Christmas, so I have a bunch, but they're all back in New York."

"I'm sure there are places to find ornaments around," he said dryly. "No one's going to miss a chance to sell as much as possible during the season."

"What I'd really like is lights. Lots of sparkling lights. Then I can turn the tree on at night and enjoy the colors."

"That can be arranged."

"Can you have lights on your tree?" she asked.

"Sure if I plug into the electrical system. LED lights don't draw much power."

"Then you're the one who needs ornaments," she said.

"I like your idea of lights only. Let's try it out. If the trees look like they're missing something we can always add ornaments later."

"Good compromise," she said with a teasing voice.

Dave stopped by their table.

"How was the diving?" he asked.

"Great. We even took some picture. It was a super spot," Shelly said with a bright smile. "Want to join us?"

"Naw, thanks. I'm meeting Phil and Bart. We're planning a trip to the Dry Tortugas in a week. Weather holding, of course."

"We'll be by tomorrow to refill the tanks," Beau said.

"I'm open at seven. See ya."

He nodded and moved on to a table on the other side of the wide deck.

"I should have checked to see if you wanted to go diving again," Beau said.

"I'd love to. I never get my fill."

They'd both ordered the Captain's Platter and when their meals came their plates were piled high with shrimp, crab, scallops and clams. Conversation stopped as they began to eat.

Shelly watched as Beau seemed to really enjoy the food. The place was a favorite of hers, but not as elegant or fancy as the restaurants he used to frequent in New York. Should she have suggested a more up-scale place?

No, she thought as she took another bite. When in Key West, do as the natives. If he wanted something different, he could say.

When they finished, they walked back along the route Beaut had taken. The tree lot was closed when they reached it.

Shelly looked over the makeshift fence.

"There aren't a lot of trees left."

"Not surprising this close to Christmas. But there are several small ones that would be perfect. We obviously need to come tomorrow when he's open—which according to his sign will be at nine."

"But he's open until six, so we go diving first and then get trees," she said.

"True. Okay, then. I'll walk you home."

"You don't have to. It's not far from here but out of the way to get to the hotel."

"I'm not letting you walk home alone. It's a nice night for a walk," he said, reaching for her hand and heading in the direction of her house.

"How do you remember where I live?" she asked as they strolled along.

"Good sense of direction. I need it sailing where there are usually no visible landmarks to get bearings from."

"Just water."

"Right. Where here there are lots of landmarks. I recognize that shop with the T-shirts pouring out."

She laughed. "Half the shops on the island have T-shirts for sale on the sidewalks. Not a very distinctive landmark."

"This is your street, isn't it?"

"It is. Lucky guess I think."

Shelly was totally aware of Beau and her hand in his. She could feel the warmth from his body even though the evening breeze was cool. She couldn't remember the last time she'd been with a man who'd wanted to hold hands. She liked it. But wasn't sure if she was making too much of it or not.

She'd never been part of Beau's dates in New York. Maybe he held hands with all the women he took out over the years.

She didn't think she wanted to ask him but she could wonder.

"I'll meet you at the dive shop at seven, shall I?" she asked when they reached her door.

"I'll pick you up. I have the tanks. We'll wait for Dave to fill them and be ready to take off."

She smiled and slowly withdrew her hand.

To her surprise, Beau leaned forward to kissed her gently.

She blinked, gazing up at him in astonishment. Licking her lips, she didn't know what to say.

Apparently taking the silence as consent, he leaned over again and kissed her–deepening the kiss slowly as if to give her time to object.

Shelly had no intention of objecting. She stepped closer and wrapped her arms around his neck as he pulled her into a warm hug. The kiss continued.

When he pulled back slightly, she felt the cool night air brush against her heated cheeks.

"Umm, good night," she said, and turned to enter her house before her knees gave way and she sank into a puddle.

"Good night," he replied.

Shelly leaned against the door trying to hear his steps as he walked away. She heard nothing over the pounding of her heart.

Beau Charlmers had kissed her!

And it had been fabulous!

She danced across the room and back again. Her heart skipped a beat and pounded.

Then reality returned.

"He probably kisses everyone good night," she said aloud, coming to a halt. "Tonight was my turn."

Still all the times she'd been his plus one at events, he'd never kissed her before. Did it mean something? Or was it the island romance seeping in?

"Who cares? I liked it and if he wants to kiss me again, I'm all for it," she said defiantly.

11

Shelly was waiting on the sidewalk in front of her house when the taxi arrived the next morning. She jumped in and greeted Beau and the driver.

"Another lovely day," she said as they sped toward the dive shop.

"Weather forecasts thunderstorms this afternoon," Beau replied. "I think we'll only get in one dive this morning. I thought about trying for that wreck Dave told us about yesterday, the Maria Eleana. I've never explored a sunken ship before."

"Sounds good. I saw one from a distance a few months back, but we didn't explore it."

"This one's not too deep so we should be okay."

Before long they were underway toward the coordinates Dave had given. The sky was cloudless, the breeze brisk, and the sea slightly choppy. But the sailboat slid through the water with a gentle rocking.

When they reached the location, Beau was

careful to stop some distance from the exact spot so the anchor wouldn't damage the sunken ship. He launched the dive buoy as well.

The ship hadn't broken apart when it sank, though the mast had snapped off about ten feet above the deck. It was covered with sand and barnacles and looked ghostly to Shelly's mind.

They swam around it, giving it a wide birth. Small fish darted through the openings.

When Beau swam to the old-fashioned spoke wheel, she watched as he gently stepped on the deck. A cloud of sand puffed around his flippers and then settled again. When he reached out to see if the wheel would turn, she swam closer. It seemed safe.

The wheel didn't budge.

She swam beside him and reached out to touch one of the spokes. She knew nothing about this ship, but suspected it was one of the Spanish ones that used to ply the Caribbean. Probably sank three hundred years or more ago. Amazing that it still looked intact, but if the wheel was anything to go by, it was still a sturdy ship. She would have expected the wood to have rotted away by now.

Beau explored the deck, poking his head in through an opening at one point, but not venturing any further.

Shelly swam around the perimeter, then looked at the sea bed. They weren't down very far, maybe only fifty feet. Surely there would be nothing left to scavenge after all these years. It was a popular spot for visiting divers and had been since its discovery several decades ago.

A canon protruded from a hole in the side. She swam closer and studied it, wondering if the ship had fought pirates and been mortally wounded. She needed to see if Dave knew more of the history of the Maria Eleana.

When they broke the surface some time later, Shelly was smiling.

"That was great. Much better than the ship I saw a few months back. That one was pieces scattered around. I wonder if it's safe to swim inside?"

"I wouldn't want to risk it, but it was interesting, wasn't it. Did you see the canons?"

"Yes, did you see any damage that would have caused it to sink? I wondered if pirates had fired upon it or something."

"There could be damage on the side it rests on. It wasn't totally upright."

They swam to the boat and soon had their diving gear off.

Beau studied the western sky for a moment.

"I believe the forecasts are accurate, look at the clouds building over there."

Shelly nodded. "I saw them. Guess we need to head back."

"We can eat lunch on the boat at the marina. Let's get underway."

The wind had picked up but was at their back for most of the way, skimming the boat across the waves. The ride wasn't quite as bumpy as it would be were they tacking into the waves, but still rocking. The quiet in the marina was immediately felt.

Once they were tied up, Beau opened the picnic basket he'd obtained from the hotel.

Today there were roast beef sandwiches, Waldorf salad and an almond cake dessert.

Shelly ate with relish, hungry after their dive.

"Unless you relish buying a wet Christmas tree, we may not make it today," Beau said glancing out a porthole at the gathering clouds. Thunder could be heard in the distance.

"I guess not."

She didn't want their day to end. But what could they do in the rain?

"Want to see a movie?" she asked.

He looked at her for a moment, then slowly nodded. "I don't think I've been inside a theater in close to twenty years. Too busy."

"I don't know what's playing but we can check it out," she said fishing out her phone from her tote.

"There's an action adventure one. That might be good. Or here's a kid's one that looks promising."

She looked up and grinned at him.

"Let's try the action adventure. What time?"

"Time enough for us to make it if we leave now." She wrinkled her nose. "But I don't want to sit around in a wet bathing suit all afternoon. We could make the three o'clock show."

"Good plan."

Beau picked her up via taxi after they'd had time to change. It had begun to rain and Shelly ran from her house beneath a large umbrella. She closed and shook it quickly when getting in, then closed the door.

"Glad you didn't have to walk in this?" Beau asked.

"I sure am. I would have had wet shoes all afternoon, but at least they wouldn't be itchy like dried salt water can get. It is really raining."

A bright flash of lightening lit up the sky with a crashing thunder roll almost immediately following.

"Not good weather to be walking around anyway," he said.

The theater was only partially full. Beau bought a big bag of popcorn for them to share. Once in the darkened theater, they found seats and soon were munching on the popcorn.

The feature started and a short time later the popcorn was put aside.

Beau casually reached for her hand.

Shelly felt her heart rate increase. She gave him a sideways look, but he seemed fully focused on the screen. Hoping she could concentrate on the unfolding plot, she tried to ignore the warmth of his hand, the tingle of awareness that swept through her. It was going to be a long movie.

When they walked out of the theater after the film, the worst of the storm had passed. A steady drizzle however continued to make outdoor activities a problem.

"Want to have an early dinner at the hotel?" he asked as they stood beneath the narrow awning.

"I'd like that."

Anything to prolong their time together. She'd had a wonderful day. Tomorrow it was back to work. And she still had no idea how long he'd be in Key West.

When they arrived at the hotel, it was buzzing with activity in the lobby. The rain continued and so make-shift conversations areas were set up as well as a traveling bar.

"I hadn't expected so many people to be here. I'll check on reservations at the main restaurant," Beau said.

Shelly paused and said, "I"ll just pop into the restroom and freshen up. Meet you back here."

He nodded and continued.

She brushed her hair, put on some fresh lipstick and stepped back into the lobby, standing to one side so she wasn't in anyone's way and people watched.

Most of those in the lobby were tourists on vacation. Despite the rainy weather she didn't notice any angry or disgruntled people. There was conversation and laughter as if they were all on an adventure.

Maybe any disgruntled guests had retreated to their rooms.

A group of women burst into the lobby shaking rain from their hair and laughing. One wore a short white veil clipped on the back of her head. A pre-wedding party with the bride, Shelly thought.

She looked at the laughing group and realized she recognized several of the women. She'd even met a couple at events with Beau back in New York. Not that they'd likely remember her. She didn't move in their social set.

They moved as a group crossing the lobby and talking and laughing. Shelly couldn't help smiling. They looked like they were having a great time.

She spotted Beau leaving the restaurant.

She watched as one of them broke away from the group and dashed over to him, linking her arm with his. She recognized Elizabeth Wilson. She remembered sending flowers to her for almost six months. Then that relationship, like the others before her, had fizzled out.

Almost as if choreographed the other women changed direction and soon he was surrounded by the laughing group.

Shelly continued to watch as he chatted with them for some time. Finally disengaging his arm from Elizabeth's, he nodded toward Shelly. Every woman turned to look at her. She smiled, wondering if she should walk over and join the group. Even as she considered it, Beau began to walk toward her.

"We can eat in about an hour," he said when he reached her.

"Fine. You had quite a group there," she said, glancing at the other women. They had continued their way to the bar.

"Suzzie Backer's bridesmaids and friends celebrating. She's getting married here in a couple of days."

"I hope the weather is nice for her special day."

"I'd suggest we get a drink at the bar, but I'm not interested in running into them again."

"There's a family bar around the corner. It's mostly special drinks for kids like a Shirley Temple, but they do offer grownup drinks as well. The only thing is there might be a lot of kids there because of the rain. They also have videos of cartoons constantly running."

"Let's give it a try. Can't be worse than a bunch of women laughing."

"I resent that," she teased. "I might want to laugh."

He nodded, pretending to be serious. "One at a time I can handle."

She laughed.

"Oops."

He shook his head. "Lead the way."

12

The family bar was only half full. The place was larger than the bar off the lobby. Walls on three sides, the fourth side was wide open facing the beach. In sunny weather one could take advantage of the large outdoor patio with chairs and tables. Inside there were low chairs for children, standard chairs for their parents, some tables, some beanbag chairs and a bar along one side that was decorated in familiar cartoon characters.

Shelly waved to the bartender. "Hi Steve, okay for us to be here?"

He nodded. "Sit anywhere."

"That table over there looks as far from the kids as possible," Beau said, nodding toward a table near the edge of the open area.

The rain continued now as a steady drizzle.

"I'll just have a soda," she said. "That way I can have wine with dinner."

"I'll get the drinks."

She wandered to the table and sat down. Today

was turning out to be better than she'd expected when she heard of the rain. And she was gratified that Beau wanted to spend more time with her. If he's tired of her company, the rain would have been the perfect excuse to curtail things. Instead, he'd asked her to dinner.

"Here you go," he said, setting down a colorful plastic cup with a little paper umbrella on top."

She laughed.

"Fancy."

"They cater to kids, obviously. I could have also gotten you a curly straw, but thought better of it."

"Aw, I might have liked that."

"I can go back and get one if you like."

She shook her head.

"No, thanks. This is fancy enough."

She plucked the umbrella from the glass and took a sip.

"What was your favorite part of the movie?" she asked.

"The motorcycle chase, of course," he replied.

They discussed the various aspects of the movie, some of which really stretched credibility, and the parts they enjoyed.

The conversation segued into books they'd read. Beau had read more than Shelly over the last few months.

"Not a lot to do for entertainment on a boat in the middle of the sea," he said.

"Where as I thought I'd catch up on reading some of my favorite authors but I'm so busy that I usually manage a few pages before falling asleep each night."

"Maybe you should take up sailing, spend a weekend on the water with plenty of time to read."

"Maybe, but then I'd want to be diving or napping. I probably wouldn't read much more than I do now. And I'm certainly not complaining. I'm happy here."

"Never think of leaving?"

"To go back to New York?"

"Or anywhere?"

She thought about it for a moment. He'd asked that before. She'd given a flippant remark but now realized he really wanted to know.

"I don't envision myself anywhere but here if I think about it. But I've only been here for about fourteen months. After I've been here ten or fifteen years, maybe I'll feel differently."

He was quiet for a moment, studying his beverage.

"Are you thinking of going back?" she asked. "To New York?

He looked at her.

"No. Not back to New York. I've discovered I can do without snow and sleet and ice and traffic and all the down sides of the city. Though I do miss seeing some of the Broadway shows."

"You can always fly back for a weekend, do the town, and then return to wherever you've docked your boat."

"True."

"Hi, Shelly. What are you doing here? You don't have any kids," a friendly woman stopped by their table.

"Hi Janie. No kids, but the other bar was crowded so we took a chance on this one."

Janie smiled and looked at Beau.

"Oh, this is my friend, Beau," Shelly introduced. "This is Janie Norris. We work together, sort of."

"Nice to meet you. As she said, we work together, well actually we job share sort of. I have the opposite concierge shifts. And two nights a week. Sometimes we cover for each other."

"And why are you here this late? It's not one of your late nights," Shelly asked.

"Danny's somewhere around here. I wanted to finish up on another excursion for a wedding party. Steve said he could hang out here. There's Danny, entranced by the cartoons."

Shelly looked over at the little boy who appeared mesmerized by the cartoon video.

"Did you come here just to hang out?" Janie asked.

"Beau's staying here. We have reservations at the restaurant."

"Oh, nice. I wish I had a friend staying here. Well, I've got to go. See you," Janie said. "Nice to meet you Beau. If you stick around I'm sure we'll run into each other again."

"I'll look forward to it."

Janie directed a look at Shelly and winked then turned to walk to her son.

"You surprised me introducing me as a friend instead of former boss."

"Would you rather I said former boss? I figured that would lead to questions and before you knew it, your cover would be blown."

"Cover?"

"Except for the bridal party, no one knows who you are. You aren't throwing money around or bragging, so I figured you wanted to keep your identity on the down low."

"Incognito?"

"Exactly."

"It makes for a change," he said thoughtfully.

"I know. I know how everyone fawned over

you in New York. Here my friends don't know who you are and so they treat you like everybody else."

"I am like everybody else," he protested.

"With a bank account with more zeroes than most people have socks."

"It's only money."

She nodded. "For some people, that's everything."

"Not you," he said softly.

She shrugged. "I like money as much as anyone else–for what it can do. If I had enough, I'd buy my little cottage outright. I'd cut my hours and do more diving. Maybe volunteer at the local animal shelter."

"Whoa, where did that come from?"

"One of the guys who works the pool side bar volunteers. He says he can't own a pet in his apartment, so he gets his animal fix by working with the dogs and cats."

"What about people?"

"What about them?"

"Ever think of a volunteer group helping people?"

"Like the food bank or soup kitchen at Thanksgiving?" she asked.

"Or more. Say working with kids who need big sister or big brother."

She looked at him thoughtfully.

"Is that something you do?"

He shook his head. "Not yet. But I've been thinking about something like that. Being on my own so much this past year has really given me food for thought on all different directions. My mother struggled when I was growing up. I had no father in the picture. Kids need a balance. I regret now not doing more when I was in New York."

"You could open a sailing school and give underprivileged kids sailing lessons. Or diving , or fishing lessons. And still live on your boat."

"Then I'd have to be in one spot for a while."

"And you don't want to?"

"Let's say I'm thinking of the possibility."

Shelly wondered if he'd think of Key West as a possibility.

He glanced at his watch. "Time for dinner, ready?"

Dinner passed quickly. The conversation ebbed and flowed as the appetizers and main meal appeared. When they were finished, Beau suggested an after dinner drink at the grown up bar, as he put it.

"One, then I have to go. I have work tomorrow," she said, reluctant to have the evening end.

The bar was less crowded than earlier. The bridal party was still in full force at several tables that had been pushed together.

Beau guided her to a quiet spot as far from the noisy party as the bar allowed.

"I hope this isn't a mistake," he murmured as the waiter approached.

"No, we're fine," she said with a smile.

She could tune out the noise and focus on Beau alone.

She wished it wasn't raining. She'd love a quiet walk home with him at her side. Especially if the moon was out illuminating everything with its silvery light.

Would he hold her hand the entire way?

Kiss her good night?

Because it was raining a quiet walk home was out of the question. When she had to leave Beau called a taxi and gave the driver her address and paid in advance. He held the door for her and brushed his lips across her cheek before she climbed in.

"I'll see you tomorrow," he said.

"I'll be at my desk," she replied, wishing she had more time off.

"I can still stop by."

He closed the door and the taxi pulled away from the hotel.

Shelly glanced over her shoulder as they rounded the corner. Elizabeth Wilson had come out of the hotel and was standing beside Beau.

Frowning, she settled in the seat and faced forward. Whatever Elizabeth wanted was nothing to do with her.

Still, she wished Beau had accompanied her home. Instead he was probably joining the ladies from New York and partying until late.

Shelly arrived at work a little earlier than usual. She got a coffee from the employee's lounge and took it to the concierge desk. There were several notes from Janie about planned excursions that day. At least the weather had turned and it was again sunny and warm—despite being so close to Christmas.

Last year she'd gone home to upstate New York and enjoyed a white Christmas. This year she was staying put. Maybe she'd walk along the white sandy beach and pretend it was snow.

An assortment of colorful flowers in a wide vase appeared.

"Shelly Alexander?" the delivery man asked, setting them down on her desk.

"Yes. These are lovely, for me?"

He nodded. "Have a nice day."

She smiled as he left. Searching in the bouquet she found a card. She already suspected who the flowers were from. Sure enough she immediately saw Beau's bold handwriting.

I'll pick you up for lunch, we'll get trees, and tonight we can decorate. Beau.

She smiled. Today wouldn't be all about work.

Right when her lunch hour started, Beau crossed the lobby heading in her direction.

She grabbed her purse and placed the Out-To-Lunch sign prominently on her desk.

"Ready?" he asked.

"Yes. I wondered if you're still getting a tree."

"I will, but we'll decorate yours first because you have lights at your house," he said as they went out front to catch a taxi.

"You'll have to decorate yours alone, then, in the daylight."

"We can do it tomorrow at your lunch hour," he said easily.

She grinned. She loved being with him. And was delighted he seemed to want to spend time with her as well.

The Christmas tree lot was scruffy and barren. There were few trees left and most of them were sad looking.

"We waited too late," Shelly said as they walked up an aisle with only two trees leaning against the fence.

"We'll find something. How about this one?"

He stopped beside a tree that looked as if a chainsaw murderer had attacked the tree.

"Are you serious?" she asked.

"You're looking in the wrong direction. I want a small tree for the boat, we'll have the guy cut off the top three feet. That part looks full and still feels hydrated."

She studied the upper portion of the tree. He was right, if the bottom five feet were cut away it would be a lovely little three foot tree.

"Will he cut it do you think?"

Of course he would. Beau could get almost everyone to do what he wanted.

"Yes. Now let's look for one for your place."

"I want a small one like yours. I don't have that much room, but could put it on a table in front of the window so it can be enjoyed inside and out. So I'll only look at the top half of trees."

Before her lunch period was over, they'd picked out the two trees. The seller assured Beau he'd have them both cut by the time he came back from taking Shelly to work.

"You don't have to do that. I'll catch a taxi and you can stay here until they are ready."

"Okay. I'll drop yours by your home and take mine to the boat. Pick you up after work."

"Deal. See you then."

13

Shelly looked forward to the evening. She'd still have to stop somewhere to pick up lights and ornaments, but then they could order pizza in and decorate her tree. She wondered if she had any Christmas music on her device. If not, during a lull in the afternoon, she'd see about downloading some so they could have music while decorating.

Elizabeth Wilson stopped by the desk in midafternoon.

"Have you seen Beau around?" she asked Shelly.

"Not recently."

Elizabeth scanned the lobby and then turned back.

"If you see him, ask him to give me a call. Or my dad. He has our numbers."

"I'll make a note of it," Shelly said, jotting down on a notepad.

"I wonder if he's on his boat. Do you know where it's docked?"

Shelly knew, but she had learned discretion long before her job as concierge.

"Sorry I don't have that information,"

To give out, she added silently. If Beau wants you to know where he's staying, he'll tell you.

Elizabeth looked at her watch again and sighed. Then turned and walked away.

Shelly was impatient for the workday to end so she and Beau could decorate her tree.

What fun it had been at the tree lot. She was impressed with his idea of cutting a larger tree to size. She hoped they could find some cute ornaments to decorate with. Much as she wanted lots of lights, she believed she would like some ornaments. She knew he wouldn't have any either.

Promptly at four thirty, Shelly tidied her desk and took the note from Elizabeth Wilson for Beau. She'd make sure he got it, though she did hope he wouldn't want to change plans because of it.

Beau was waiting outside when she walked out.

"Hi," she said, her heart rate increasing.

"Hi," he said. "I have a taxi waiting. I took the liberty of buying some ornaments and lights. I hope you'll like them. Figured it'd save time."

"Great idea. I can pay you back," she said as she slid into the cab and across the bench seat.

"No need," he said getting in beside her.

"I thought we could order pizza in. I made some cookies last night before bed so we can have them with ice cream for dessert."

"Sounds good."

He gave the cab driver her address and sat back.

"Oh, this is for you," Shelly said, taking the note from her purse.

He glanced at it and shrugged, crumpling it up and tucking it into his pocket.

"Not urgent, then," she said.

"Hardly."

When they reached Shelly's cottage, she noticed the plastic bags stacked on the side of the small porch and her tree already in a stand.

"Good, nothing was stolen," he said with satisfaction when they walked up the walkway.

"It's a nice neighborhood, but still, it's lucky nothing was taken."

She felt almost as excited as she used to when she was little and anticipating Christmas morning.

Once inside, she kicked off her sandals and put the bags on the dining table, rummaging through them and withdrawing the ornaments and lights.

"Oh, they're perfect!" she said, holding up a box of glittering ornaments.

She exclaimed over another one and then the lights.

"You remembered I wanted lots of lights," she said in delight at the strands and strands of small lights.

"It wasn't hard to remember, you told me a couple of days ago," he said dryly.

He enjoyed watching her expressions as she opened each of the bags. Christmas ornaments weren't that exciting to him, but someone might think they were made of gold for the joy they seem to hold for Shelly.

Little things made a difference. Inexpensive things could bring happiness.

He'd learned to do with very little over the last year, food and fuel for the boat. Books had been a necessity. But for the rest of societal must haves, he'd done without just fine.

"First we have to test the lights," she said, handing him a box of lights and opening one herself.

"They should all work, they're brand new."

"True, but we test before we put them on the tree just to make sure," she said.

"Family tradition?"

"Yes, and no matter how careful my mom was when we took down the tree each year, we'd always find some tumbled and tangled and it would take hours to get them all straightened out. So remember that part when we take down the tree."

She stopped suddenly and looked at him with stricken eye.

"Sorry, I didn't mean to assume you'd still be here or want to help take it down."

He wanted to tell her he wasn't going anywhere yet. But some of that really depended on her when he broached the reason he was in Key West.

"No worries. I'm happy to take the ornaments off the tree when the time comes. My time is flexible."

"Well, then, good."

She seemed flustered and he wasn't sure why. They'd worked together for years. He thought he knew her, but was coming to find that she wasn't the open book he'd expected when he arrived in Key West.

He liked getting to know her on a personal level. But his hopes were still in the plans he had for the future. He'd thought when he first arrived that she'd jump at the chance he'd offer when he brought it up. However, seeing her in her new life, meeting her friends, he wasn't sure any more.

He didn't like that. He liked making plans and having everything fall into place. On the other hand, business ventures rarely progressed in a straight line, so he was prepared for a wiggle or two.

They called for pizza once the lights had been examined.

Then Shelly began to wind them around the small tree. Beau handed her another strand and watched as she studied what she was doing. When she was finished she asked him to plug in the lights.

The tree sparkled with colors of every shade from the lights.

"Perfect," she said with a happy smile.

He nodded, watching her as she gazed at the tree.

She looked at him with her wide smile, then it faltered a little.

"It looks nice, don't you think?"

"Perfect as you said," he replied never taking his gaze from hers.

Again she seemed flustered. Beau pushed it a little.

"And the tree's nice, too."

She narrowed her eyes. "Are you flirting with me Beau Charlmers?"

He tilted his head slightly. Was he?

"And if I am?"

"Totally unexpected. What do I do?"

"Flirt back?" he suggested stepping closer and cupping her face in his hands.

Slowly so she could stop him if she wanted, he lowered his face to hers until his lips brushed across hers. She smelled so sweet. Her skin felt so soft. Her eyes were unfocused when he pulled back.

"Well, wow," she said a second later. "Totally unexpected."

"I'm not your boss any more," he said softly. "Though that could change."

"What?"

"Nothing. I'll explain later. In the meantime, ornaments?"

She stepped back and he dropped his hands, turning to reach for the first box of ornaments.

Handing them to her, he was surprised when she skimmed her hands over his before taking the box.

He met her look and smiled.

She was up for flirting and so was he.

From then on he did his best to touch her whenever it wasn't too blatant. Reaching around her to place an ornament he brushed her shoulder. Handing her another ornament, he let his fingers linger for a second. Once he offered to help her and covered her hand with his as together they hung an angel ornament.

She giggled and turned. Taking advantage, he brushed his lips across hers again.

The doorbell rang.

Pizza timing sucked, he thought as he crossed the room to get their dinner.

He paid for the pizza and carried it across to

messy table. Pushing aside the bags and boxes, he set it down.

Shelly had gone to the kitchen to get paper plates and drinks.

Soon they sat on the sofa and began eating.

"Too bad it's so warm," he said. "It'd be a nice night to have a fire in a fire place."

"If we were back in New York. Houses here don't even have fireplaces," she said. "That part is fun at my parents' home. Oh, I forgot."

She jumped up and went to her phone. Plugging in speakers, she looked at him. "I have a play list of Christmas carols which should have been playing while we decorate."

The familiar carols began to play softly in the background.

"Now's when we need that fire in a fireplace," she said sitting back down.

When they finished eating, Shelly gathered the paper plates and pizza box and trashed them.

"Before we have dessert, we have a project," she said, pulling a package of popcorn from her cupboard.

"And that is?" Beau asked, rising from the sofa and walking to Shelly.

"Stringing popcorn, of course. What respectable Christmas tree would be complete without a garland of popcorn?"

"The tree looks nice as it is," he said, glancing back at the sparkling lights reflecting in the ornaments.

"It does, but it'll look even better when we have our garland. And we'll make enough for you to decorate your tree the same."

Once the popcorn was ready, Shelly brought out needles and thread and soon they were both stringing the fluffy kernels.

"No, fair. You can't eat the popcorn, it's for the decoration," she fussed at one point when Beau took a handful to munch.

"You sound like my mom," he said with a laugh.

"Well of course if you're going to eat the decorations."

He laughed again and began to thread as many kernels on the needle as he could.

"We're not in a race," Shelly commented when she noticed what he was doing.

"If you're going to do something, do it right, fast and efficiently."

"Whoa, that's your business motto, right?"

"Something along those lines."

"This is supposed to be fun not fast and efficient," she protested.

"I am having fun. I can do it quickly."

She grinned and shook her head. "Fine, your garland will be finished before mine."

They worked in companionable silence for a while, listening to the Christmas music.

Beau declared his finished at the ten foot mark. Shelly decided to end hers though it was only seven feet long. Still, for a short tree it would do.

She carefully wrapped the garland around branches enjoying the added embellishment to her tree.

"Now it looks perfect," she said, stepping back to study the tree.

14

She brought out the cookies, but Beau declined the ice cream saying he was still full from the pizza.

They sat side by side on the sofa and munched the chocolate chip cookies quietly.

"You made these you said," Beau said.

"Yes."

"They're really good. My mom used to make these for special occasions. We didn't have a lot but she did her best. Tonight has brought her memory back in full force. I miss her."

"I bet you do. I don't know how I'll cope when my mom passes on. She's healthy and only middle age so I'm hoping she'll be around for another 40 years, but still we all only get one mom. I'm happy if tonight was special for you."

Shelly's phone rang. She answered it to hear Janie's voice on the other end.

"What's up?"

"My childcare fell and broke her ankle. She's not going to be able to watch Danny for at least a week, until she can get a walking cast. I've got some friends who can stay with him, but not tomorrow. Can you cover for me tomorrow night? It's my night to work and I know it means a double shift, but I'd really appreciate it. I hate to miss any work this time of year."

"Yes, I can. I'm sorry she was injured. Let me know if I can do more."

"This is plenty. I owe you."

"Maybe buy me a latte one day. Danny's okay, right?"

"Yes, though he ended up going to the emergency room with Tessa. When I got the call I thought he'd been injured too. Fortunately not, but I still had to go to the hospital to pick him up. He's fine. Thanks again for tomorrow."

"Problem?" Beau asked when she shut off her phone and slipped it back into her purse.

"Janie's babysitter broke her ankle so she's scrounging around for people to watch Danny while she works and has it covered except for tomorrow, so I'll take her shift."

"That makes it a long day for you, two shifts."

"It does, but evenings are usually quiet, so I'll

be okay."

Beau rose.

"I'll head out so you can get as much rest tonight as you can in preparation."

She wanted to protest, but it was getting late. Much as she loved being with him, she didn't want to be cranky tomorrow for a double sift.

"Thanks for the tree, decorations and dinner," she said walking him to the door.

"Thanks for the memories and the garland," he held up the bag with his popcorn garland.

He opened the door and turned back to her, reaching out to tilt her face up to his.

"I had a good time. I always seem to with you."

He leaned over and kissed her.

Shelly wanted to grab hold and never let him go, but she refrained.

He ended the kiss and studied her face for a moment before turning and walking away.

She closed the door, bemused by the entire evening. She couldn't wait for the next time they were together. Every time was special. And she was falling more and more in love with the man Beau was. He seemed more relaxed than ever before. It was fun to see this different side of him.

He could spend his time with anyone he wanted–and he was spending it with her!

There were people lined up at the concierge desk the next morning when Shelly arrived. The day promised to be perfect–sunny and warm. Guests were excited to explore all the island had to offer and wanted the best spots laid out for them.

Shelly handed out packets of what to see and do, answered questions, called for reservations, and pointed out places on maps. It seemed as soon as one group finished, two more showed up. She loved talking about her new home, but was looking forward to a slow down sometime before dark.

Finally shortly before she'd grab her lunch she had a lull. Looking around the lobby she couldn't believe there wasn't someone heading her way. Leaning back in her chair she exhaled a long breath. The morning had been hectic. And today she was doing double shifts. If it was that busy in the afternoon, she might not make it all the way through to nine.

Now, instead of being swamped, she had no one. Replenishing the packets of what to see and do, she straightened the display next to her desk with individual brochures from the various sites in Key West.

When it was time for lunch, she wandered over to the snack bar to get a bowl of clam chowder. Beau had switched their day to decorate so she could devote today to her job.

She'd eat at one of the tables by the beach and watch the guest enjoy the water.

Shelly was almost finished when Elizabeth Wilson stopped by her table.

"So did you accept Beau's proposition?" she asked. "I'm trying to get him to come with me to Suzzie's wedding as my plus one, but he said he still has business with you."

"Excuse me?" Shelly said. "I don't understand."

"The job offer. When we had breakfast this morning he was talking about a new venture he's very excited about. And he wants you in as a key role. I remember you now, you were his right hand in New York. You even attended some of the charity events with Beau. Being a concierge in a hotel has to be a huge come down. Did you leap at his offer?"

"He didn't make an offer. I still don't know what you're talking about."

"He said he came here to make you a job offer. That's clear, isn't it?"

Elizabeth sounded as if she was explaining something to a five year old.

"Good grief, I can't believe he hasn't gotten around to it yet," she said. "At breakfast he said he had some loose ends to wind up. Once that's settled, I'm sure he'll be available for Suzzie's wedding on Christmas Eve."

"I'm sure his free time has nothing to do with me," Shelly said.

She felt slightly sick inside. Had Beau been spending time with her to butter her up for a job offer? She'd wondered if he'd grown tired of sailing. He was too dynamic to retire from life in his thirties.

"Well I know that. You two don't move in the same circles at all. But he's most annoying with being vague about what he has planned. I haven't seen him in more than a year. We have a lot to catch up on."

"I'm sure you do."

Shelly rose and gathered her bowl and napkin.

"If you'll excuse me, I have to get back to work."

"Fine. If you see Beau, tell him I'm looking for him."

"I'll do that," Shelly said in as polite a tone as she could manage.

Inside her heart was breaking. Had the dreams she'd dared dream been nothing more than foolish wishes?

She freshened up, splashing cold water on her face, trying to ignore the roiling emotions that Elizabeth had cause.

When she thought about it, it was unlike the man she'd known in New York to spend time with her without some business connection. Had he come to only to offer her a job?

Then why hadn't he made his offer?

He didn't need to take her scuba diving or decorate a Christmas tree or eat meals together.

He certainly didn't need to kiss her.

She sat down at her desk and gazed sightlessly across the lobby. Her heart ached. There was no other way to explain it. She'd loved the time they'd spent together. She thought he'd enjoyed it as well. She had even dared to hope it meant a new direction between them.

Now it seemed as if it merely was a ploy to get her to accept some job. Hadn't he brought up her feelings about Key West more than once? Was he trying to gauge her willingness to relocate?

She wasn't going to do it. She liked her current job and living here. She didn't consider it a come down from what she'd done in New York, but a life choice. She had friends, activities to do she never could do in New York. Her life was settled. If he'd tired of the sailing scene and wanted to start up a new company he could. Offering her some new high powered job wasn't tempting enough to disrupt her new lifestyle.

She wished now that she'd taken things slower around him. Wished she hadn't felt so delighted in his company.

The next time she saw him—what? Should she confront him? Or wait for him to bring it up? Or should she take the initiative and refused to see him again?

The afternoon seemed to drag on and on. She was half worried she'd see Beau and not know what to say and half anxious to see him to find out what was going on.

She hoped she hadn't made her feelings known. She wanted some secrets to stay that way. They'd said goodbye in New York, she could say goodbye again.

But she didn't want to.

She wanted his affection and attention to

develop into something more. Something they could build a future on.

Shelly ordered room service for her dinner, eating it in the children's bar. She was avoiding Beau—in case he looked for her—but she didn't care. She was going to make it through the evening shift and then head for home. She wanted to go to bed and pull the covers over her head and forget every word Elizabeth said.

The evening passed without incident and the moment nine o'clock arrived Shelly was out the door. She'd ridden her bike to work and was glad for the exercise getting home.

Her cottage was dark. She rolled the bike up the walkway and parked it on the porch where last night there'd been a tree and decorations.

She blinked back tears.

Letting herself in, she tried to ignore the tree. Walking straight to her bedroom, she quickly got ready for bed and climbed in. Flicking off the light, she lay in the darkness reviewing every moment she and Beau had spent together.

If he wanted to offer her a job, why hadn't he? There'd been plenty of opportunities. And she knew from working with him for years that he wasn't shy about pushing ahead to get something he wanted.

The next morning Shelly arrived at work wary about seeing Beau. He'd known she was busy all day and evening yesterday, but would he try to see her after work today?

There was an envelope on her desk with her name written in bold letters. She recognized the handwriting. Did she want to open it?

Fortunately, people started coming to ask for her help. She shoved the envelope into her purse, put it away and began helping the hotel's guests find the perfect activity for the day.

At her break, she escaped to take a stroll along the water's edge. She kicked off her sandals and let the spent waves cover her feet as she walked. She'd brought the envelope and opened it once she was alone.

"Dinner tonight? My place? We can trim my tree then. I'll pick you up when you get off work."

It was signed Beau.

She would have loved to spend the evening on his boat–before. They'd talked about decorating both trees together, but her heart was no longer in it. She'd rather go home and read a good book.

Maybe she could leave early and be gone when Beau showed up.

Once back at her desk she called Janie.

"Any chance you could come in a half hour earlier?" she asked her co-worker.

"Sure. Problems?"

"Personal ones. I'd really appreciate it. You were able to get people to watch Danny, right?"

"Yeah, we're covered for the week and then we'll see how Tessa's doing."

Shelly couldn't walk away without giving Beau some excuse or he'd follow her home. She wrote a short note saying she had other plans for the evening and left it at the concierge desk with his name on the envelope.

Too bad there wasn't another volleyball game tonight. She'd relish something else to focus on.

When Janie arrived, Shelly quickly told her about Beau's expectation of seeing her tonight but hoped her note would put him off.

Her friend promised to give it to him as soon as she saw him.

Taking another exit from the hotel, Shelly was taking no chances in running into Beau if he arrived early. She rode her bike home, then stashed it behind her house. If he did swing by, he'd think she was still away if he didn't see her bike.

Entering, she quickly made a sandwich and then went to her bedroom to eat. Lights on inside the house would also give her away. She pulled the shades in her room and sat at her small table eating. When she was done, she turned off the light and turned on the television.

Attuned to any activity outside, she didn't know whether to be relieved he hadn't come by to see if she were home or wishful that he had.

Reviewing their activities, she knew she'd misconstrued anything special between them. He'd never said anything about becoming a couple, or of seeing each other exclusively, or even any mention of their friendship enduring beyond the next few days. She still didn't know his schedule but before long he'd be heading out.

At one point she switched off the television and turned on the lights. She was being silly. She didn't need to hide from Beau. Next time she saw him she'd tell him she wasn't interested in changing jobs and wish him well.

15

The next morning Shelly showed up to work resolute in her determination to say goodbye to Beau if he came by her desk. She was pleased to find a group of people waiting knowing that focusing on her job would make time fly and the guests would act as a buffer if Beau showed up unexpectedly.

By mid morning she was convinced he wasn't coming. While disappointed since she'd prepped herself to cordially say goodbye, she was also secretly relieved that the moment of confrontation hadn't yet arrived.

She saw women from the wedding party gathered together and heading out somewhere. From their attire, she thought they might be going shopping. Certainly not to the beach. If she had a cold New York to return to when leaving here, she'd make the most of the beach. Different stokes for different folks.

It was almost lunch time when Beau stopped by her desk.

"Lunch?" he asked, smiling confidently at her.

"Sorry, I've made plans," she replied avoiding his eyes.

Plans to eat alone, but he didn't need to know that.

"Okay, how about I pick you up after work and we have a quick dinner and then decorate my tree?"

She opened her mouth to refuse, then closed it. Maybe it'd be better to be more private to hear out his real reason for seeking her out. And then when saying goodbye.

"Okay. I get off at four thirty today. Too early for dinner."

"Okay, so we'll decorate first?"

She glanced at him and gave a nod.

"I'll see you then."

She watched him walk away. She could look at him all day. Even the back view.

Tears stung her eyes. She blinked them away. She'd tell him goodbye tonight.

At least they'd have one more evening together.

Or should she tell him after they decorated the tree and skip dinner which would could prove to be very awkward. Or skip decorating and get right down to things?

She remembered what he'd said about his Christmases as a boy. She could help decorate his tree to set the stage for another Christmas to remember. She could do it.

Naturally the day seemed to crawl by after that. No one sought concierge services. She tidied everything twice and still was bored to tears. Mixed with trepidation about the evening and anticipation to spend a few more hours with Beau, the afternoon dragged.

Finally it was four thirty and prompt as ever Beau walked into the lobby.

She picked up her purse and went to meet him.

"Ready?" he asked.

They caught a taxi and were soon at the marina. It was already dusk and the overhead lights were on.

Once on the sailboat, she put her purse down and looked at the tree. He had set it up on the back bench, so it was higher than the sides so to be visible from all around.

"Lights first," he said, drawing out a bag which held lights and ornaments.

"Same deal here, test them first," she said, reaching for one box. "Where's the power outlet?"

He pointed to where they could plug in the lights.

"Battery power," he said.

They tested the strings and found one that didn't light up.

"We have enough without this one," he said. "Good call to test first."

Shelly nodded and began wrapping her lights around the tree. The joy she'd experienced with her tree was missing tonight.

"You're quiet," Beau said at one point.

She looked at him wanting to challenge him about why he was spending time with her, but not yet. She shrugged.

"Something bothering you?" he asked.

"We can talk at dinner. Or maybe after dinner?"

He put his string of lights down and took hers from her hands.

"That sounds ominous. Let's talk now. What's on your mind?"

She pulled her hands away and stepped back. Not much room on a sailboat to stand too far away.

"Why are you here?" she asked.

"To decorate the tree," he said.

"No, I mean in Key West? Why here? Why now?"

He studied her for a moment. "To see you."

"Why?"

"We worked together for years. I wanted to stop by and see you again," he said evenly.

"No other reason?"

He hesitated a moment and Shelly felt her heart drop.

"There is something else. I thought we could talk about it later but if you want to talk about it now, fine by me. I'm starting up a new venture and want you to be a part of it."

"I like my job here. I'm not interested in getting back to the business world we had in New York."

"It's not like that."

"It doesn't matter. I'm not interested."

"You haven't even heard what I'm planning," he said leaning a little closer. "It won't be anything like Farmington. It'll be more—"

She reached for her purse.

"I'm not interested. Sorry. I need to leave now."

"Wait. What? We haven't finished the tree and then I have dinner."

She faced him.

"I'm glad you stopped by Key West in your travels. It was good to see you again. Have a nice life."

She turned and stepped off the boat to the dock and hurried away.

Beau stared after her in astonishment. What had just happened?

He hadn't even had a chance to tell her about his plans. And what was that have a nice life comment about? He wasn't going anyplace—at least not without Shelly.

He took off after her.

By the time he reached the street she was gone. There was no taxi in sight so he began walking. A convenient aspect about Key West was its size. He could easily walk to her house and maybe come up with a reason for her reaction along the way.

Something was wrong and he wasn't sure what it was, but he'd find out. They'd had a wonderful time since he arrived. What had changed?

She apparently had known something about the job offer even though he hadn't broached the subject yet.

He remembered talking about it with Jason Wilson at breakfast yesterday. With Elizabeth sitting right there. Had she told Shelly? But why would she? They weren't friends.

Hands in his jean pockets he walked steadily. Her house wasn't that far from the marina. He hoped she'd gone home. Maybe they could still have dinner together and talk this out.

Unless—he didn't like the thought she might not wish to see him again—job offer or not.

She had to know there was more going on than a job offer. So maybe she did and this had been her way to back off and let him know there was no future together.

He wasn't going to take that as an answer unless she told him point blank. He was a straight shooter, didn't dance around things but was forthright and honest. And he knew Shelly was, too. If so, she needed to tell him exactly what was going on.

It took him almost forty minutes to walk to her cottage. The lights were on he noticed as he walked up to the small porch. He knocked on the door. He hoped she'd answer.

16

Shelly opened the door. She stared at Beau. She hadn't expected him to follow her home.

"May I come in?" he asked.

She hesitated then nodded and opened the door wide.

He reached out and caught her hand in his, closing the door and pulling her gently into the living room.

"There's been a misunderstanding," he said.

He sat on the sofa pulled her down beside him, her hand still in his.

"I like my job, I'm not looking for another one," she said.

"You said that already. Fine. I'll look elsewhere for my startup. But that is not the only reason I came to see you. The simple truth is I missed you."

She blinked then frowned as if not understanding.

"Think about it. We worked together for nine years. Worked in tandem. You knew as much about the operations and plans of Farmington as I did. You did your best to grow the company. We worked long hours. We went to events together. Someone even called you my work wife one time because you kept track of all events in my life personal and business."

She nodded. Her gaze never left his.

"The thing is at first I loved sailing. I could truly relax after being years and years going full blast to make it. And the end goal always seemed just beyond the next horizon. How much is enough? I finally decided to do something else. I have more money than I can burn through in a lifetime. That drove me to change directions. So going where the whim took me, taking time to do nothing was amazing. I felt better than ever before."

She nodded again.

He wondered if she'd say something but she kept quiet.

"Then gradually I found myself feeling lonely. I didn't have any close friends. I knew a lot of people in New York, but no one I could sit around and talk with, or even not talk to but be with someone. And every time I had that feeling I'd think of you."

"Me?" she squeaked.

"Yes, you. So I thought I'd come to see you. To see if that relationship we enjoyed was still viable, still something we could do again. Initially I wanted you for my new start up–wait before you say anything–you were clear in turning me down. Without even listening to my proposal I might add. But it doesn't end there. At least not for me."

"But–"

"Shh. These last few days have been what I've been seeking. Spending time with you, talking like we used to, doing things together. I haven't felt lonely once. Even back at the boat or my room, I had more time together to look forward to. I've had a good time."

"Social life down here is nothing like what you enjoyed in New York," she said.

"It's not like my lifestyle in New York, more like what I had before I made my first million. Money can't buy everything. It couldn't buy my Mom back. It couldn't change my childhood after I was grown. Soon it became a game–how much more can I make if I do this or try that."

"Nice game. You won. You are one of the world's wealthiest men."

"And lonely until I saw you again. Another thing money can't buy is true friendship. Someone who likes me for me and not for my money or what my money can do. While I haven't gotten to know your friends here very well, those I've met so far have shown no signs of fawning over me or hitting me up with some fantastic deal that would make us both money."

She smiled at that.

"I think everyone here likes living in Margueritaville. They aren't out to make a fortune. For what? So they could live in Key West and kick back? Though I see your point about being liked for yourself and not your money."

"Anyway, I want to spend Christmas with you. No job offer. No ulterior motive. Well, maybe one."

"Which is?"

"I like you Shelly, I always have since the first day we met."

She smiled. "I like you, too, Beau."

It was do or die time.

"I want more," he said.

Her eyes grew wide. "Like what?"

"Like maybe love?"

She stared at him as if she'd never seen him before.

"Love?" her voice squeaked out again.

"And marriage," he continued.

"Marriage," she repeated.

"Doesn't have to be right away. We can get to know each other better, spend more time together–"

Before he could finish his sentence she launched herself against his chest where his arms automatically came around her.

"Yes, I love you and have forever I think. Yes to love, yes to marriage. Yes!" she exclaimed.

He smiled right before he kissed her.

The world seem to spin out of kilter. Time seemed suspended. The world had come right.

They were both breathing fast when he broke the kiss.

Shelly snuggled up against him not believing how happy she was.

"I thought you'd be leaving soon," she said.

"No need now," he said, holding her close.

"What about your new venture?"

"What about it? I thought you weren't interested."

"Well, when I believed Elizabeth that you only came here to make me a job offer I wasn't at all interested. That changed. Now I'm your future wife. I definitely think I want to know what you have in mind."

"I like the sound of wife. How soon can we get married?"

"Soon. But so you know my mom would never forgive me if I didn't get married with friends and family in attendance."

"Fine with me. I don't have any family to worry about. Would Valentine's Day be too soon?"

"Tomorrow wouldn't be too soon," she replied, touching his chin with her fingers. "But that's impossible. I'll call my to tell them and see what we can accomplish by Valentine's Day."

She looked around the room, her eyes lingering on the Christmas tree.

"I'll miss Key West," she said slowly.

"Why? We can live here if you like."

She sat up so she could see his face.

"Do you mean that? I thought you'd want to go back to New York."

"We can visit any time we want but for my new project, I can do that from anywhere. Plus there's your job at the hotel. Did you want to quit that?"

"I don't know. Tell me about your new project," she said.

"I want to build simple houses and offer them to single moms with kids, sort of like Habitat for Humanity, but for single moms. I have the money to do this and I want to remember my mom that way. She wouldn't have had to work two and three jobs if we'd had housing costs covered."

"That's a wonderful idea. I thought you were thinking of something along the lines of another Farmington. I'd love to work with you on something like this."

"I've thought about this a lot over the last year and you are the only one I could think of when I considered who I'd want to work with. We'll be starting off slow. Lots of start up areas to cover from building the homes to how we select the families. We were a terrific team at Farmington, I know we'll be a terrific team with this."

"I can't believe you told Elizabeth before asking me," she murmured.

"I didn't. Not deliberately. Jason and I were discussing it at breakfast the other day. I think she was there, listening I guess. She did say something, didn't she?"

"She told me to hurry up and give you the answer on the job offer so you'd be free to go to the wedding with her. She seems to think I'm holding things up."

He frowned and shook his head.

"Elizabeth and I dated briefly a couple of years ago as you know. Short and then done. I like her father but that young woman is determined to marry money and doesn't care much who she has to marry to achieve that."

Shelly doubted the other woman would find marriage to Beau a hardship.

"If you said no, if you refused to see me ever again, I still would not have gone to that wedding with Elizabeth Williams," he said in no uncertain terms.

"So I guess I give notice tomorrow."

"If that's what you want. I figured we wouldn't start in earnest until the first of the year."

"I'll tell my boss tomorrow. I think there's a bit of a lull in January after the holidays, so they'll have time to find someone else. Are you serious about staying here in Key West?"

"Absolutely."

"I have some really good friends here. You've met a couple. I've been invited to a party tomorrow night. Come with me and meet some more. And I'll show you off as my brand new fiance. Dare I tell them I've been in love with you for almost nine years?"

"Sure, make me look like a real slow poke to take so long to ask you to marry me."

"Thanks heavens for sailboats is all I have to say."

He smiled as he kissed her.

"I think my feelings for you have been there all along . Being apart brought them to the forefront."

"Mmmm, maybe. I don't really care how you realized you love me, just that you did."

"With all my heart and soul. I don't ever want to be apart again."

She snuggled back against his chest.

"So are we going to be house hunting or will we live on your boat?"

"What's wrong with this place? At least until the kids start coming."

"Kids?" she said, sitting back up again and looking at him.

"Sure, don't you want some children?" he asked gazing deeply into her eyes.

Gazing back Shelly knew she'd love to have a little boy who looked exactly like his daddy. And a little girl with his dark hair who would likely wrap him around her little finger.

"Yes, I'd love to have some children with you. A houseful."

He put her beside him on the sofa and went on one knee on the floor.

"I want to do this right," he said. "Like my mom would have wanted me to. Shelly Alexander, would you marry me?"

"Yes, thank you, Beauregard Charlmers, I'd be honored."

She grinned at him but her expression changed

when he brought out a ring box from one pocket and opened it, showing her the lovely solitaire diamond ring.

"I've had this for months, hoping I'd get up the courage to ask you and hoping you'd say yes," he said, taking the ring and putting in her finger. "I love you, Shelly."

She couldn't imagine him needing courage to do anything. He hadn't made all his money without taking humongous risks.

She looked at the ring on her finger, moving her hand so the light caused rainbows to appear.

Then she looked at him. "I love you, Beau. I always have and I'm sure I always will."

Shelly arrived at the resort shortly before nine the next morning. She felt like she was floating on air. Each time she glanced at her left hand she smiled again. She loved the ring. Her mom and dad had been surprised when they'd Zoomed last night before Beau left.

They were delighted to meet Beau and begin discussions on the wedding once they heard the news.

Shelly's mom gave her a list of things to get started on from locating a venue, to finding a florist, to begin looking for a dress. In the meantime, when her parents mentioned getting airline reservations and seeing who else in the family could attend the wedding, Beau offered to charter a plane for everyone. They were thrilled.

Shelly looked around the lobby. She loved this job. It had seemed almost like play rather than work. Not that she was sad to leave. Getting married to Beau was the most amazing thing to ever happen to her. She'd loved him in secret for so long, she could scarcely believe he'd fallen in love with her. And working together as he planned would be even better than anything the resort had to offer.

Tonight many of her friends would get to meet Beau. She hoped he'd come to enjoy their company as much as she did. Eventually people might find out how wealthy her husband was, but she hoped not until he knew who were his true friends.

A florist deliveryman walked over to her desk carrying a large bouquet of tropical flowers in bright yellows and deep reds.

"Alexander?" he asked setting the display on the desk.

"Yes, thank you."

She grinned at the lovely bouquet and hunted around the flowers to find the card.

It was from Beau, but she knew that.

I'll pick you up for lunch. We have a tree to decorate. She tucked the card in her purse and hoped the morning would fly by.

It was close to noon when Shelly began watching the entrance. She'd given her notice earlier that morning. Her boss wasn't happy she was leaving, but expressed her happiness that Shelly was marrying the man she loved. She hoped the wedding would be at the resort.

Something to discuss with Beau. Neither one of them had thought about the details of a wedding.

Shelly brought out her purse and put the out to lunch sign on her desk just as Elizabeth Williams and her father entered the lobby from the outside terrace. Jason headed for the elevators, but Elizabeth changed directions and walked over to Shelly.

"Well, did he ask you?" she demanded as soon as she was close enough for Shelly to hear her.

"Actually he asked two questions."

She smiled.

"I hope you said yes. As soon as he gets business out of the way he'll be open for some social activity I hope. You did say, yes, didn't you?"

"I said yes to both," Shelly said.

She caught sight of Beau coming in from the front and smiled beyond Elizabeth.

"He's here now," she said.

She looked at Elizabeth.

"But he's not going to go to the wedding with you," she said firmly. "He's taken."

"What?" Elizabeth looked totally confused.

"Hello, sweetheart," Beau said walking up to Shelly and kissing her. "Ready?"

"Yes. I was telling Elizabeth that you can't go to the wedding with her. You're taken."

He laughed and put his arm around her shoulders turning to look at the other women.

"Too true. Shelly agreed to marry me. Our own wedding will be on Valentine's Day. Tell Suzzie I wish her all the best."

"You are engaged?" Elizabeth asked, appearing stunned.

Shelly held out her hand with the sparkling diamond.

Elizabeth turned to walk toward the elevators.

Beau urged Shelly out to the front where he had a cab waiting.

"That actually went better than I expected," Shelly said as they sped to the marina.

"What, Elizabeth?"

"I think she was really hoping you'd go with her to the wedding."

'The only wedding I want to go to is ours. And I'm starting to think Valentine's Day is too far out."

She laughed.

"I want to enjoy being engaged. I've never been before and don't plan to be again," she said.

"There is that. What do engaged couples do?" he asked.

"Spend time getting to know each other better, plan their future, and have lots of fun."

"Christmas is the best time to start then. I believe this will be my best Christmas ever," he said, kissing her gently as the cab sped to the marina.

"This will be my best Christmas. But who know what the future holds for us," she said a minute later, grinning up at him. "When we have all those kids you were talking about."

"I can't wait!"

If you liked A Key West Christmas,
you'll love **A Teaspoon of Mistletoe** from my
Sweet Clean Christmas Romance Collection.

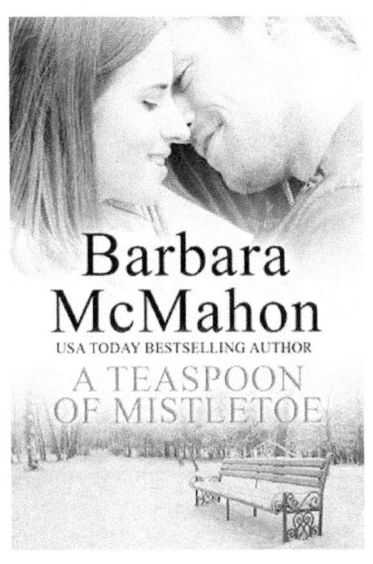

If you enjoyed **A Key West Christmas,** please
consider leaving a review.

For a complete list of Barbara's books, please visit
www.barbaramcmahon.com.